THE AFRICAN DESERT: 1942

Rommel's Afrika Korps sliced deep into British territory, aiming its dagger-thrust straight for the lifeline of the Suez Canal.

Somewhere behind the German lines was the fuel dump that fed the racing Nazi war machine. To find and destroy that source, a special breed of fighter was recruited from the prisons, the dives, the pestholes of the Middle East. Thieves, perverts, murderers, it did not matter. For in this impossible mission, the only thing that counted was the supreme ability to

PLAY DIRTY

PLAY DIRTY is presented by Harry
Saltzman for United Artists release. A
Lowndes Production, the film stars Mi-
chael Caine and co-stars Nigel Daven-
port. Also starring are Nigel Green, Harry
Andrews, Aly Ben Ayed and Vivien
Pickles.

Produced by Harry Saltzman, directed by
André De Toth, screenplay by Lotte
Colin and Melvyn Bragg, based on an
original story by George Marton, the film
is in Technicolor® and Panavision.

PLAY DIRTY

by

ZENO

A DELL BOOK

Published by
Dell Publishing Co., Inc.
750 Third Avenue
New York, New York 10017
Dell ® TM 681510, Dell Publishing Co., Inc.
Printed in the United States of America
First printing—March 1969

PLAY
DIRTY

THE RE-EQUIPPED *British Eighth Army lay ready to strike from its prepared positions, stretching from the Mediterranean, west of El Alamein, south to the lip of the impassable Qattara Depression. Ten divisions along sixty miles of front and, waiting for them to strike, General Rommel, his Afrika Korps and the Italian Desert Army.*

Three weeks earlier, Rommel had made his last desperate bid to break through to Alexandria, Cairo, and the Suez Canal. His Panzer divisions had struck in the south, crashing through the lightly held forward positions of the 8th Army, driving forward in what was intended to be a great encircling movement aimed at cutting the British lines of communication running to the east, capturing their petrol dumps and supplies, severing the great Suez artery, and laying the way open for a future offensive into southern Russia.

The attack had been smashed by Montgomery's tanks and artillery, waiting on the Alam Halfa Ridge for the Panzer divisions to turn north, and the Afrika Korps had been forced to withdraw, much of its armor shattered and its precious petrol wasted.

Between the opposing armies, in the narrow strip of desert which separated them, patrols from both sides probed and stabbed at forward positions, took prisoners, and sought any scrap of information which might be turned to effective use. And from the British lines more ambitious blows were struck at Rommel's desert airfields by motorized patrols from the Long Range

Desert Group, the SAS, and other groups so irregular as to be unknown outside the headquarters of Special Forces, Middle East. Aiming at objectives far out in the desert, sometimes hundreds of miles behind the German lines, failure and death were more often the result than success.

CHAPTER 1

THE JEEP came across the desert from the south. Driven fast, it raced over the broken ground, its mudguards hanging on by shreds of metal and wire, its broken exhaust fighting a losing battle against the volume of the radio turned up to full blast in the back of the vehicle. The tune was "Lili Marlene," the singer, a woman, and the words, German. The throbbing beat of the music and the throat-catching stridency of the words surged out from the jeep over the emptiness of the Western Desert till at last they were lost in the unending sameness which surrounded the bullet-riddled vehicle and its two occupants.

The driver of the jeep, Leech, sat slackly in his seat, his hands clamped tightly on the wheel, fighting the slur and drift of the desert floor. His eyes, red-rimmed and sunken, glinted a defiant reply to the challenge of the blazing sun; his hair, grey-yellow-floured by the wind-borne sand was as matted and thick as the hide of a sick animal, and his lips, cracked by the heat and browned by dried saliva, were gelatinous and ridged. They were drawn back against his teeth, so that his mouth showed contradictory expressions. On the one hand, there was a challenging contempt for the opposition of man and the elements but, on the other, the licking tongue and overstretched lips betrayed the pain and discomfort of exhaustion. The German officer's cap, worn in the style made popular by the Afrika Korps, complemented the condition of the vehicle he drove.

With his eyes still fixed on the open desert in front of him, he half turned and spoke to the man sprawled in the seat beside him.

"Well, you're a tedious young gentleman to travel with. I always find that your type make the most boring traveling companions."

He turned further round, and his eyes switched from the desert to the face of the other man; he laughed out loud into the marbled face of the dead British officer heaving stiffly in the passenger seat.

Leech swung back till he was again facing the open desert in front of him, and his brow furrowed for a fleeting second. Soon he would be back. He laughed again, the sound unforced and content. You couldn't have everything.

His face changed suddenly, a snarl replacing the sardonic grin. Far ahead, in the desert, his red-rimmed eyes had spotted the first signs of military civilization. As he drove on, his speed unaltered by what he had picked out in the distance, his eyes selected, detail by detail, the environs of an army checkpoint.

He took one hand from the wheel, jerked off his German officer's cap and tossed it into the back of the jeep. It fell softly, cushioned by other German trophies —a German signpost, a brand new pair of German binoculars, a German record player and a number of records. He groped under the seat till he found an English officer's cap. He stuck it on his head, deliberately very straight and pulled down over his nose like a guardsman's. He dropped his hand to the radio and changed the station to a British one. A nasal, slightly cockney voice sang to him, "You are my Sunshine." He spat dryly out of the side of the jeep and raised his eyes in mock sadness. He spoke again to the rolling corpse.

"All good things have to come to an end. Two's

company but. . . ." He broke off as he approached the checkpoint where the military police, alerted by the sound of his engine, had taken their eyes off the east-west road and turned them south to the open desert out of which he was driving.

He hit the road only a hundred yards short of the checkpoint, driving in fast, braking at the last moment. A corporal of the military police stepped forward smartly. "Papers please, sir."

"What do you want, my driving license?" Leech put all the contempt he felt for the regular army into his question as he handed over his papers. He jerked his thumb as the corporal flicked through them. "I don't suppose you want to see his, do you?"

The MP handed Leech's papers back to him and looked down at the dead officer: his face tightened a fraction but he said nothing. Instead, he stepped back, saluted, and waved the jeep on. Leech drove past him, laughing on a note that made the corporal shiver slightly in the sun.

The compound, lying in the center of a small Arab village twenty miles to the east and south of El Alamein, was to a casual eye more disreputable, dirty and disorganized than the village around it. In every part of its limited space, men were working on shattered vehicles, gun-mountings, and the other impedimenta of desert war. They laughed often, and shouted one to the other in languages as assorted and strange as the clothes they wore. Although they moved about their tasks without haste, every movement of their hands, each jerk of their heads revealed a barely suppressed urgency, a high-strung desperation.

The rickety, hanging doors of the compound burst apart with a grating crash under the thrust of the jeep, and Leech drove fast through the opening he had forced. He stopped the vehicle in the center of an open

11

space, and for a second rested his head on arms crossed over the driving wheel, but almost at once he sat up, the token gesture of tiredness dismissed.

As he cut his engine, all other sound in the compound ceased; men laid down their tools, watching with careful, cagey eyes the jeep and its two occupants, the living and the dead. Leech eased himself out of the driver's seat and then stood very still, supporting himself on the hood, his mouth twisted and cynical and his slitted eyes turned towards a door in one of the dilapidated buildings.

The ragged blanket doing service as a curtain was pushed aside and Colonel Masters stepped out, pausing for a moment, blinking in the glare of the sun. He was a tall man, sloppily dressed in civilian clothes, his trousers as crumpled as a prewar undergraduate's; he wore an unbuttoned cardigan, leather-patched at elbows and cuffs, and his sockless feet were encased in Arab sandals. He was unshaven. He paused briefly, his face calm, only his clear, unmilitary eyes appearing mildly perturbed. He walked on slowly towards Leech followed by a young staff-captain, smart and spotless in his tropical service dress. Leech watched the contrasting figures as they approached him, calculating the strengths and weaknesses of each: Masters he knew completely, Attwood, the young staff-captain, hardly at all, and that mostly by hearsay. The colonel he could handle because he knew him, and because Masters needed him. Attwood mattered only because he had the ear of Brigadier Blore who commanded Special Forces.

Masters and Attwood faced him, filling the only gap left in the circle of silent men standing round the bullet-riddled jeep. Masters spoke, his enquiry concerned but falling short of accusation.

"What happened to Karinski? And the two Maltese, and Achmet?"

Leech shrugged and spread his arms wide, forcing his lower lip outwards.

"I brought the young officer back as you told me. I left the others behind."

Masters looked down at the body of the dead man, and without raising his head glanced sideways at Blore's staff-captain, gauging his reaction. He feared Attwood more than Leech did, for he knew better how precarious had become the very existence of the unit he commanded. He looked again at Leech.

"What went wrong this time?"

Leech met his glance wearily, bored by the need for explanation.

"We got within twenty miles—then got spotted by a brace of Stukas."

Attwood spoke for the first time.

"And what happened to Lieutenant Evans, exactly?"

Leech shrugged again.

"He was just unlucky."

Masters looked quickly at Attwood, sensing before seeing the disgust and distaste written on the smooth cheeks and in the immature eyes. He decided it would be better to talk to Leech later and alone.

"We'll talk when I get back. Get yourself cleaned up."

Attwood looked at his watch, a little obviously.

"Brigadier Blore will be waiting, sir."

Masters looked at the close-shaven face, and then down at the shining Sam Browne and glittering buttons of Attwood's tunic. His face showed real expression for the first time. A dour acceptance of an unpleasant chore, something to be done, but to be got over with quickly. He walked over to Attwood's jeep, standing outside the building which housed his office.

Attwood watched him, his mouth half open in disbelief.

"You're not going to change, sir?"

Masters climbed into the passenger seat of the jeep before replying. He sat down, looking straight in front of him, his hands clasping a bundle of maps, and his lips pulled tight, showing the first sign of impatience.

"Change? Into what?"

They drove out through the open doors of the compound, Leech and the silent group around him watching them, contempt for Attwood and his kind plain on all their faces.

Leech motioned to two of the unit to take the body out of the jeep. They pulled him forward and then out. The dead officer finished up face downwards, held by three men, a bloodstained gash showing in the back of his khaki-drill shirt. His carriers looked down at the slit, recognizing not a bullet hole but a stab wound. Leech followed their gaze, unconcerned. He spun his finger in front of him, gesturing to them to turn the body over so that the wound would no longer show.

They carried the body away without reverence. It was something which was no longer of any use. Beyond repair, it was of less value than a twisted gun-mounting or a jeep with a broken half-shaft. In their hands, it lost even that shred of dignity that the dead command.

Leech thrust his hands into the pockets of his trousers and strolled away from the scene. He did not swagger, but there was an arrogance about him as strong as the hooked nose jutting from his sand-encrusted face.

CHAPTER 2

THE DRIVER of the jeep brought it to a smooth standstill outside Brigadier Blore's office, and Masters and Attwood climbed out.

Blore sat behind his desk, leaning back in his chair, his hands flat on the tidy surface; his clean-shaven, soldier's face stern and unyielding. His bright blue eyes stared aggressively at Masters as the colonel halted in front of him and gave his open-fingered, civilian salute.

Blore maintained a deliberate silence and, waiting for him to speak, Masters found himself thinking, not for the first time, what calculated ham-actors so many senior officers were. Perhaps it worked when they were addressing troops, but Masters thought that the dullest of the undergraduates he was used to teaching would have seen through the pose to the man behind it.

Blore looked up at Masters, playing for effect. He knew Masters had twice his intelligence and one hundredth part of his military knowledge. He knew that to Masters the war in the desert was near to being an academic exercise. He was aware of Masters' background: a don; a professor of ancient history at Cambridge; a man who believed that the basic principles of desert war had not changed in over two thousand years, and that the same principles could be applied as effectively today; one who saw camels, horses and tanks merely as the cavalry arm and was convinced that those who knew the desert and the history of the wars which had been fought over it would always triumph over those who knew less of tried and proven principles.

Blore chose his moment, after the pause he considered just long enough, and a tone he would not have used to another officer of Masters' rank.

"Another one down the dilly. So far, Masters, you've cost the British Army forty-two thousand pounds in what you call 'miscellaneous costs,' plus seventeen jeeps, twenty-four trucks, a small fortune in ammunition and supplies—and the lives of three British officers."

Masters' reply was deliberately deferential, almost an agreeable aside.

"Forty-three of my own men have been killed as well, sir."

Ignoring the loss of hired, alien killers as being of no consequence, Blore continued as if Masters had not spoken.

"Your total requisition for the past twelve months has been one hundred and twenty-four thousand, five hundred and sixty-three pounds. You've sent eight missions behind the German lines—and you have achieved nothing. Colonel Masters, you are a luxury we cannot afford."

Masters spoke quietly, groping among his maps as a don might who was seeking the written authority for something he had propounded.

"My work over the past twelve months has been a preparatory exploration of the techniques which I intend to employ. The experience of so many commanders of the past who have fought over this terrain will ultimately prove invaluable."

Blore answered flatly, his voice showing more clearly than his words that no matter how many times Masters might reiterate his views, he, Blore, disagreed with them.

"Modern warfare has nothing whatever to do with the activities of Alexander the Great, or Hannibal."

"The principles of desert warfare do not change."

Blore's voice became harder, more aggressive.

"The principle of getting value for your money hasn't changed either, Masters. Your unit is disbanded —as from now!"

With one hand awkwardly sorting his maps, Masters appeared not to be listening. With difficulty, he snapped open his briefcase with the other hand and took out a number of photographs, spreading them on the desk so that Blore could see them, but the brigadier continued to speak without looking down.

"Captain Attwood will go back with you and you will hand over to him. You, yourself, will take a week's leave to find yourself a proper uniform. I know your work requires you to be in mufti, but you might shave occasionally. You will assume command of the prisoner of war camp at Qattara with effect from the seventeenth."

Unable to resist Masters' activities, Blore glanced down at the maps and photographs in front of him. At once his attention became arrested by a photograph more prominently displayed than the others. He reached out for it, compulsively, and as he examined it Masters spoke hastily.

"I have located, through contacts with the Majabra tribesmen, the perfect target for my kind of operation."

Blore's eyes remained fixed on the photograph.

"Where the hell did you get this?"

Masters was smiling now, very gently.

"It appears that the Majabra have learned how to use the Brownie cameras I supplied them with."

Too impressed to hide his interest, Blore turned from the photograph to one of the maps on the desk.

"This petrol dump is four hundred miles behind the German lines."

Masters leaned forward, his timid deference gone, showing the first signs of eagerness since the interview had started.

"Precisely. You can't get at it, but I can." His voice became firmer, carrying a new authority. "Two men are going to stop Rommel. One of them is Adolf Hitler, who cannot give him enough fuel. The other is me, because I'm going to blow up the little he has."

Blore sat back in his chair, his eyes calculating, his mind made up.

"Masters, I'm going to give you one more chance, but . . ."

Masters was again deferential, but in his eagerness he interrupted before Blore had finished speaking.

"Thank you, sir."

". . . but this time you'll have to succeed. I'm putting the expedition under the command of a British officer."

Concern, dismay, showed on Masters' face. He felt the condition imposed by Blore like a ball and chain thrown suddenly round the legs of a running man.

"But British officers don't understand my methods, sir, they always . . ."

"You'll do as I say, and this time I want him back—alive."

For a moment Masters was silenced, and he stood very still, his eyes drifting above Blore's head and his mind working quickly. A typical infantry officer would ruin the operation, imposing the kind of discipline that the men would neither understand nor accept. Leech, whom Masters considered vital to the success of the expedition would refuse to operate under a regimental officer. His only chance was a civilian in uniform.

"If I must have one, could I have somebody who

knows something about petrol installations, pipelines, that sort of thing?"

Blore nodded absently, his mind already at work on the type of insurance he intended taking against what he felt was Masters' certain failure.

"I'll see if we have someone to spare." Blore got to his feet, cutting the interview short. "Don't forget, Masters, this is your last chance."

"Yes, sir."

Masters lowered his head and started to pick up his photographs and maps, less depressed now that there was the possibility that the British officer seconded to him might be a technical expert instead of an infantry-man.

Blore reached forward and took the maps and photographs from Masters' hands. "I want to look at these. I'll send them back to you."

Masters' hands half followed the papers as they were taken from him. He opened his mouth to protest, but changed his mind in time, accepting a situation he had not the power to change. Instead, he drew himself upright into an apology of a military stance, saluted sloppily, and with a muttered, "Yes, sir," left the brigadier's office.

For a long minute after he left, Blore stood in the same position, the maps and photographs he had taken from Masters held loosely in his hand, his face, no longer disguised, showing the extraordinary, *simple* ruthlessness of which senior officers of all services are capable when to them the final objective becomes clear and necessary. He turned at last to the waiting Att-wood, standing very correctly in the background.

"Ask Watkins to step in, would you?"

The staff-captain's "Sir!," and swift departure were almost a caricature of how Masters could never be-have.

19

Blore returned slowly to his desk and sat down, spreading the plans, photographs and maps in front of him. He went over each of them carefully. At last he smiled, a twisted grimace that had nothing to do with humor, and when the knock came on his office door, his command to enter was cheerful and confident.

Attwood was accompanied by a major of the Coldstream Guards. The staff captain moved at once to his position behind and to the right of Blore's desk. Major Watkins came to a natural stop rather than halted; his brief salute managed to be both competent and casual.

Blore looked up at him from behind his desk, happy with the outlines of the plan already clear in his mind and at ease with one of his own kind. He smiled up at Alan Watkins without showing his teeth, and Watkins smiled back, a replica of the brigadier's silent greeting. Blore was in no hurry as he marshalled his thoughts and eliminated the need he felt for the kind of act he put on for those who did not think along the same lines as himself or, for one reason or another, could not be trusted with the whole picture. Watkins was an old Etonian, and as Blore understood him, he was mad, as mad as Leech, perhaps madder, but protected against the reactions of the same by his suave, civilized bearing. Watkins could kill, murder, and justify his action under the guise of military necessity in a calm unruffled manner. Leech butchered without excuse or explanation, defying his superiors to judge him.

When Blore at last spoke he broke a silence which might, between two other men, have been uncomfortable.

"Alan, I've had an idea. Look at that—and that." He threw two photographs of the huge German petrol dump on the table in front of the major.

Watkins studied them, his eyes narrowing.

"There must be millions of gallons in there from the look of things: Rommel's?"

Blore nodded, and with an extended finger pointed at a position on a map lying to one side of his desk.

"It's there. Four hundred miles behind their lines." He smiled blandly, "I've got the location pretty accurately from my Majabra tribesmen—as a matter of fact, they took the photographs for me. D'you want to go and blow it up?"

Watkins was both impressed and pleased, and for a second his eyes hooded, an instinctive covering for the manic gleam he could not suppress, but his reply was what was expected of him.

"We'll try and give you a show, sir."

Blore threw an open hand at the map.

"Rommel's here." He sliced his extended hand from west of El Alamein to the edge of the Qattara Depression. "His lines of communication are extended just about as far as they can go. If we can destroy the bulk of his fuel supplies at this precise moment—it could make all the difference."

Watkins nodded. "We'll try, sir."

Blore took a few paces away from the desk, no longer looking at Watkins, his eyes seemingly fixed on the personal realization of a dream.

"Rommel's going to be defeated by two men," he said, as if the thought had just occurred to him, "Adolf Hitler, who can't give him enough fuel, and me, because I'm going to blow up the little he has."

Behind the desk, Attwood just failed completely to control his face at the brigadier's appropriation of Masters' line. Blore continued, the denouement of his scheme apparently thrown away as an afterthought ...

"Oh, by the way, I'm sending a decoy-group ahead of you—Masters' bunch."

Watkins' head moved sharply, his brows raised in an affected expression of disbelief. "Not *those* gangsters!"

"They'll set off a day before you with the same route, the same orders. If there's any trouble, let them catch it."

An appreciative smile appeared for a fleeting moment on Watkins' face, and was gone in the same instant. He liked the idea a great deal, but he said of necessity:

"Not particularly pleasant, sir."

Disregarding Watkins' token contribution to the ethical niceties, Blore closed the conversation.

"You leave in two days, Watkins. Good luck."

As the door closed behind the Coldstream major, Blore returned to his chair. With an air of satisfaction, he said to Attwood, "Well, that's that."

The staff captain hesitated. Already lost in the ramifications of the two interviews, he was no longer sure that anything the brigadier had said was necessarily intended.

"What about the, er, British officer for Colonel Masters, sir?"

Blore looked up, his thoughts brought back abruptly by the reminder. "Completely forgot—oh—tell them to find a spare captain somewhere." And as Attwood reached the door, Blore tossed him an afterthought.

"I suppose he'd better know something about petrol."

CHAPTER 3

THE VERANDA of the Arab house overlooking the small Arab port showed that it had been converted into a British Army office. It contained the usual blanket-covered table and a filing cabinet, and from its edge, against the rail, a heliograph flashed a message to an oil tanker standing half a mile from the quayside.

The Royal Engineer captain operating the heliograph completed his message and remained still, his eyes fixed on the bridge of the tanker, ignoring the bustle of the tenders unloading their cargo of oil drums on the quay, and missing the arrival of the jeep which, driven fast by a British corporal, screeched to a standstill below him.

The corporal jumped out and approached a sergeant who was supervising the unloading of the oil drums. He spoke to him briefly, and the senior NCO turned reluctantly from his work and gestured with his hand towards the veranda and the RE captain who was again signaling to the bridge of the tanker.

The corporal dashed into the building and through an outer office, arriving on the veranda where the officer was standing, his eyes glued on the tanker's bridge.

The corporal coughed and saluted the captain's back.

"Captain Douglas, sir?"

Douglas didn't turn his head, his concentration barely broken by the corporal's question.

"Yes?"

"Colonel Hommerton would like to see you in his office, sir."

"Mmmm-hh-mm."

The heliograph on the tanker flashed out a fresh message, and the corporal waited while Douglas read it. The heliograph stopped signaling and Douglas turned to the table at his side. He looked down at the chess board and the half completed game set out on it; he reached out and moved a black knight, then stood back and appraised the new position; he nodded his head, a slow smile dawning on his face.

The corporal had followed his movements, and now he coughed nervously.

"Colonel Hommerton said immediately, sir."

Douglas continued to study the game he was playing with the captain of the oil tanker.

"Tell Colonel Hommerton I will be there in an hour . . . I have to finish unloading the fuel."

Unseen, the corporal smiled at the captain's back.

"As you say, sir."

Douglas arrived outside the office of Colonel Hommerton, the Commander Royal Engineers, just as a pretty ATS girl came out. Douglas gripped her arm and bent his head quickly.

"Ann . . ." he murmured into her ear.

She pulled away from him and looked up into his face, her eyes shining. "You're late."

"I know—what's up?"

"I don't know, honestly."

"It's not about us, is it?"

"No, no." Ann was emphatic.

"Well, wish me luck." Douglas released her arm and went in.

Hommerton was sitting at his desk, a captain whom Douglas didn't know standing behind him. He saluted, beginning to feel worried: he didn't like the look on their faces.

"You sent for me, sir?"

Hommerton didn't reply directly, but spoke over his shoulder to the captain behind him.

"Captain Douglas is on loan from British Petroleum. He worked for seven years as a field engineer with their Anglo-Iranian branch."

The captain appraised Douglas. "So you know the desert?"

Douglas looked at the other's three pips and grimaced, hesitating a fraction of a second before replying. "Yes—er—a little."

"Excellent," the captain said. Smugly, like a scoutmaster praising a well-tied knot.

Hommerton correctly interpreted Douglas' scowl as resentment at being interrogated by a fellow captain. He filled the gap quickly.

"Captain Attwood here is from HQ Special Forces. They want an officer with some experience of fuel supply to take command of a rather unusual unit."

Douglas didn't try to keep the suspicion out of his voice.

"May I point out, sir, that the arrangement with British Petroleum was that I stay in port areas."

Hommerton's head jerked up, his eyebrows raised, the astonished act of a senior officer who sees an order being questioned, and when he spoke his voice was deliberately severe.

"What are you wearing?"

Douglas paused before answering, lowering his eyes in resignation. He could see it coming. He was in for the corny, ritual humiliation.

"British uniform, sir."

"British *Petroleum* uniform?"

"No, sir."

"Good. Captain Attwood will give you the brigadier's orders." Hommerton turned to Attwood. "He's
your man."

In another office, Douglas and Attwood faced each
other, alone. Two men of similar backgrounds for the
first eighteen or twenty years of their lives, but now
dissimilar in nearly everything they thought, did, or
believed in. Douglas was the taller of the two, his fair
hair long and beginning to curl on his collar; his khaki
drill clean enough, but soft and crumpled, a silk square
tied loosely round his neck, and his suede desert boots
sun-bleached and dusty. He was a few years older than
Attwood, but his smooth, good-looking face was still
civilized, unmarked by the limiting stamp of the military code. A qualified engineer with years of practical
experience behind him, master of a constructive
profession, he had only contempt for the Attwoods of
the army. Looking at Attwood he remembered and, for
the first time, felt a genuine sympathy for Shake-
speare's Hotspur and his fury when, after a battle, he
was confronted by a popinjay of a staff officer, per-
fumed like a milliner.

Attwood stood very correctly, resplendent in his drill
service dress, his Sam Browne belt and buttons shining
and his brown shoes polished as if for a General's
inspection. To him, Douglas was a sloppy amateur,
necessary to the war effort because of his training, but
with no knowledge of or respect for army traditions;
with no Sandhurst background. He didn't even look
like a soldier.

"Well, aren't you going to give me the brigadier's
orders?"

Attwood hesitated for a moment, and then decided
to limit his information to the bare essentials. He
wasn't going to be talked down to by a thirty-year-old

of the same rank as himself, who looked and spoke with the casual insolence of an undergraduate.

"You will report to Colonel Masters at his headquarters in Sidi Azeiz. How soon can you move?"

"What shall I need to take with me?"

"Whatever a man of your experience will need for a prolonged journey in the Western Desert."

"How long?"

"Colonel Masters will give you the details."

"You're not being very helpful, are you, Attwood?"

"I'm telling you all that I am authorized to, and probably all that is necessary at this stage."

"Don't be so bloody supercilious—where am I going, and what for?"

"I told you, you're going into the Western Desert."

"There isn't much of it between us and Rommel, so it must be behind the German lines—is that it?"

Attwood's face froze at Douglas' tone. "That should be fairly obvious, even to an RE." Attwood stuck his swagger stick under his left arm. "I'll have a driver and jeep pick you up in three hours from now." He turned on his heel and went.

Douglas stared at the door, Attwood forgotten. He'd have plenty of time to see Ann after packing his kit. He walked out of the building and into the town, wondering what the hell his qualifications had let him in for.

CHAPTER 4

SITTING IN THE passenger seat beside the driver, as they hurtled forward over the desert track towards the Arab village in the distance, Douglas found it hard to think clearly. The idea of commanding what seemed likely to be a group of saboteurs had never occurred to him. His work before the war with British Petroleum had been hard, sometimes uncomfortable, and occasionally a little dangerous. But those dangers had been ones he understood and accepted as part of his job: they were also measurable, and could be largely avoided by forethought. What lay ahead of him was completely unknown. His knowledge of the desert was considerable, and under ordinary circumstances he moved about it with confidence, but this was outside his experience. A few times, he had been in areas subjected to bombing, and on an occasion, the most frightening moment of his life, he had been on the deck of an oil tanker when it was machine-gunned from the air. Before the war, there had once or twice been the threat of trouble with local tribesmen, but there had always been someone else to handle it, and it had never really blown up into a situation which the most timid would call frightening.

He glanced at the back of the jeep where his luggage heaved sluggishly at each bump in the rutted track. Was there anything he'd forgotten? Past experience had taught him to keep those possessions which had to be carted about in the desert down to a minimum, but he knew nothing about the time he would be away, the distances he would have to cover, or the situations he would be likely to encounter. He wondered what the unit that he was to command would be like: how large it was, and what type of men would make up its complement. He supposed it would be some sort of irregular commando unit. The Long Range Desert Group had their own officers and, if it had been intended that he should accompany one of their patrols, it would have been as an attached specialist—he would not have been in command. The more he thought about it, the more disturbed he became. The more consideration he gave to his position, and to the little that Hommerton had told him, the more difficult it was for him to imagine what type of formation would require one man to contribute a knowledge of fuel supply and desert conditions and, at the same time, take command of what Hommerton had described as an unusual unit. Attwood had told him very little apart from whom he should report to, and where. There had been a mutually recognized antipathy between them from the moment they had met. He had resented the young staff officer's supercilious, self-satisfied attitude: Attwood had seen this and been deliberately vague and standoffish.

He switched his thinking deliberately. He'd find out soon enough. He wondered when he'd see Ann again. Thinking of her, his loins moved, and he smiled quietly —perhaps it wouldn't be too long.

The young driver took the jeep into the village fast, weaving his way through the strolling Arabs and lurching camels with a familiarity bred of experience. He brought his vehicle to an abrupt halt in the middle of the road and in the center of the village, at a point between a café and a barber's shop. Hopping smartly out of the driver's seat, he grabbed Douglas' luggage and dumped it on the dusty road. Douglas climbed out more slowly, disbelief on his face as he took in his surroundings. As the driver jumped back into the jeep, Douglas stopped him.

"Are you *sure* this is the place?"

The driver smiled up at the officer's troubled face as he thrust at the clutch.

"This is it, sir, Sidi Azeiz—and the café's over there."

He swung the jeep round, missing a goat by inches, and tore back the way he had come, leaving Douglas standing alone amidst surroundings familiar enough under different circumstances, but impossible for him to associate with the headquarters of a military formation.

He glanced about him, at the lounging Arabs, the running children: at the barber's shop behind him where a lather-covered face showed dimly above the grey drape below it. There was not a soldier, a military vehicle, or a scrap of service equipment in sight.

He bent and picked up his kit, and behind him the barber bent and spoke softly into the ear of the man he was shaving. Leech opened his eyes and raised himself in the chair, watching Douglas as he made his way into the café. His face was without expression except for a slight twist in the corner of his mouth, but his hooked nose and out-thrust chin were like twin guns trained on Douglas' back.

Douglas stepped through the door of the café, his face calm and his doubts hidden. The Arabs in the café watched him in silence as he put his luggage down carefully to one side of the door and brushed the sand of the journey off his khaki drill. Then he picked up his kit and made his way through to the bar, ignoring the alien figures seated at the tables and drifting through the murk around him. He stopped in front of the Arab barman who leaned on the counter, his face blank and unfriendly.

"Colonel Masters?"

The barman shrugged a negation which took the points of his shoulders nearly to his ears.

Douglas put the bags carefully on the floor of the café, thinking, his lips pursed. If the confident driver had made a cock of it, he was in trouble. They'd come over thirty miles. He straightened up and spoke to the barman again.

"I'll have a beer please."

"No beer."

"Whisky?"

"No weeskee."

"What *do* you have?"

"Chay . . . TEA." The barman made the exaggerated English word sound like the curse of the prophet.

"I'll have tea."

The barman turned slowly away to heat it, and Douglas rested one arm on the counter and looked round at the same moment that Leech came through the door behind him. Deciding that from now on he'd play it off the cuff, Douglas said nothing, his own face as expressionless as the other's.

Leech came up to the bar as if Douglas had not been present. He didn't speak, but stood waiting while the barman took a bottle of whisky and poured a good measure into a dirty glass, muttering something to Leech in Arabic, out of which, to Douglas, only the word "Masters" was distinguishable.

The barman came back to Douglas and started to pour out his tea. Douglas watched him, and the dead fly which, already in the glass, rose steadily as the barman slowly poured. Douglas stole a look at Leech and noted that he was watching the fly intently, a quirk of amusement limited to his mouth. Before turning back to the barman, the tea, and the fly, Douglas took in Leech's eyes quickly. They were devoid of humor, the glint in them something Douglas failed to recognize.

At last, the tea and the fly rose to a level that satisfied the barman and he stopped pouring. Turning aside with the pot in his hand, he saw Leech's flat gaze fixed on the glass, and Douglas' look of amused disgust. With a spread smile which could have meant anything, he leaned forward and hooked the fly out of the glass with his forefinger, the performance careful to a point of meticulousness.

Douglas pushed the glass away from him, without anger, and turned to where Leech, no longer watching, had reached for his own glass. The barman and the other Arabs watched Douglas.

Leech tossed back his whisky in a single movement and returned the glass to the counter, the whole of his hand wrapped round it, so that to the watching Douglas it looked like a weapon. Leech twisted round till he was facing Douglas, the empty glass still grasped in his hand.

"You looking for Colonel Masters?"

"Who are you?" Douglas put into the question an English middle-class tone guaranteed to infuriate or reduce to subservience.

He might as well not have bothered: it was lost on Leech, or ignored by him.

"Name's Leech."

"British Army?"

Leech held back his reply long enough for his look of contempt to register. Then he spoke:

"No." He released his glass. "Follow me."

Still playing it off the cuff, Douglas said nothing, but picking up his bags he followed Leech out through a door to one side of the bar and down a corridor.

Leech turned abruptly into an opening and, following him closely, Douglas had barely time to see the name "Colonel Masters" scrawled on the outside, with its equivalent in Arabic beneath it, before he was inside a large, untidy room, Leech jerking his thumb at him.

"Some kind of soldier to see you, Colonel."

The man behind the desk looked up vaguely, his unshaven, sunburned face lost in thought, and Douglas found himself thinking of an archaeologist just returned from a hard dig. He questioned politely:

"Colonel Masters, sir?"

The man behind the desk nodded. "That's right."

Douglas sprang to attention and saluted, his boots ringing on the floor. Masters looked startled and embarrassed.

"No need for that. You'll be Captain Douglas, then. Put your stuff over there and sit down." He half turned his head to where Leech had sprawled himself in a chair, casual and at home. "My number two, Captain Leech."

Still standing, Douglas spoke, trying to be friendly. "Oh—how d'you do—which regiment, Captain?"

"Late of the Fourth Panzer."

Baffled, Douglas muttered a polite "oh" and used the excuse of seating himself to cover his bewilderment. Masters ignored the exchange.

"Know what you're here for, Douglas?"

"I understand I'm to command one of your units on a special mission."

Leech burst into a loud chuckle, head thrown back, eyes closed, his strong, white teeth appearing to leap outwards from his mouth in derision.

Masters turned to him with a gesture as near to impatience as he could probably achieve. "Thank you, Leech."

Still chuckling, Leech got to his feet and made his way towards the opening in the wall, undisturbed by his dismissal. As he passed Douglas, he held the other's eyes for a second.

"See you later." The words dropped from Leech's mouth—spaced—and Douglas felt in them threat and promise. For long seconds, he and Masters sat listening as Leech's chuckles changed to a ringing laugh which grew fainter as he wandered down the corridor and away from them.

Masters spoke first.

"An excellent man."

Douglas felt that the colonel would have used the same tone and adjective to describe a rare map. He made Leech sound like a specimen.

"Is he always like that?"

For the second time in a few minutes, Masters chose to ignore an opening. Instead, he reverted to the purpose of Douglas' posting.

"Let me explain exactly what you're here for." Before continuing, he walked over to a map on the wall, and getting to his feet Douglas followed him.

Masters pointed to an area already marked with a cross.

"Leptis Magna." He paused, savoring the sound. "It is a Roman port in Cyrenaica that the Germans appear to be using as a petrol dump. We are here." He pointed to a spot east and south of Alamein.

Douglas peered closely at what he took to be formations marked west of where he knew the British lines to be.

"Are these Rommel's positions?" he asked.

"No." Masters paused, lips pursed and eyebrows raised. "These are the positions of the Carthaginians in the year two hundred and fifteen BC."

Douglas felt his collected calm slipping away from him. Every minute spent with Masters or Leech brought with it a sense of wild improbability. Masters continued, recognizing Douglas' reaction for what it was.

"Desert warfare hasn't changed. We are in much the same situation as Sayed Al-Bhin, when he was being driven back—here and here." He pointed at the map.

"Sayed Al-Bhin, sir?"

"Although he is little known, Sayed was a great military genius, one of the foremost exponents of the art of desert war." Masters' eyes took on a yet more unseeing look, and Douglas, the corners of his own eyes crinkled in perplexity, realized that to the colonel the present campaign and those of the past were academic exercises. Masters spoke with the quiet authority of an academic lecturing a class.

"Now what exactly did Sayed do? Well, first of all he concentrated the bulk of his army in unassailable positions between the Qattara Depression and the sea to hold up the enemy—which is pretty much what we've done. Then he sent an expedition to the south," Masters drew a route with his finger, "down to the Qattara Depression, across Qattara, through the cliffs at the Siowa Pass, west across the Sand Sea, north over the Stone Desert, and crash into Leptis Magna, where the Carthaginians were holding their supplies—just as Rommel is."

Masters' eyes came back to the present, and he gripped Douglas' shoulder with enthusiasm.

"And that's what you're going to do."

Douglas looked at him in disbelief. He turned to the map.

"I'm going to lead a unit down there, across there, over there, and up there?"

"Exactly. I'll give you my best man. He knows the ropes."

The certainty to whom the Colonel was referring made it sound to Douglas like the preliminaries to be carried out before a medieval death sentence. His question was a flat, resigned statement of fact.

"Captain Leech?"

"He has considerable experience." Masters looked at Douglas from under his brows. There was something not quite right about his manner, something at variance with the little Douglas had learned of him. Colonel Masters was playing a game, and he was aware of what he was doing.

Douglas stood for a long time looking into Masters' eyes, appalled by everything which lay ahead of him. He saw himself trapped by the necessary disciplines of the service into carrying out a lunatic operation, directed by a mad professor, in the company of a raving psychopath. He found himself wondering what the other members of the unit would be like.

"Let's go outside and have a look round." Masters' voice was conciliatory, in some way a compensation for the series of shocks he had dealt Douglas. Douglas smiled a rueful acceptance of the invitation, and he followed down the corridor, through another door in the back of the café and out into a strange complex of buildings lying within a walled compound.

He stood beside Masters on a raised step at the rear wall of the café, only listening with half his mind as the colonel pointed out and explained to him the workings of what was, at one and the same time, a billet for troops (although Douglas saw not a man he would have recognized as a soldier), an armory (containing every type of small arms used by the three armies in the desert conflict) and a vehicle repair shop (which gave the impression of relying largely on the efforts of an enormous smith who swung his hammer trapped between the twin glares of the forge and the sun). As Masters talked on in his donnish voice, diffidently claiming credit for himself, or apportioning it to another for some particular innovation, Douglas summed up his own position as he saw it. He could refuse the command and return to his own headquarters, relying on his connection with British Petroleum and the guarantee the Army had made to his employers about his military employment to keep him clear of a court-martial, or he could go through with the operation. The temptation to follow the first line was strong, and the added incentive of Ann and their nights together made it nearly irresistible. Opposing a course he thought both rational and justifiable there was only his upbringing and all he'd been taught about duty and a soldier obeying orders. He wondered how right the teachings really were, and whether in fact he, a civilian seconded to the army, could seriously be considered to be a soldier in the real sense of the word. He had almost decided to refuse the command when his eyes settled on Leech, one of a small group of men standing in a loose circle, their eyes held by something on the ground. The tight-lipped, ironic smile and the contemptuous set of the strong face were enough to tip the scale. He had to go, and when the cards were finally on the table it had to be he who was really in command.

Masters stepped down and strolled towards the group, Douglas at his side. As they got nearer, they could both see through a gap in the ring of men a small circle of fire, about eighteen inches across, and a scorpion inside it rushing desperately from point to point in an effort to find a way out from the threat of the flames.

As they drew up to the watching group, Douglas looked at Leech's face and saw—understanding. Leech knew exactly how the scorpion felt, and as the scorpion, defeated by the closed circle, retreated to the center and stood poised with its sting held over its own back ready to strike, his face assumed an expression of sympathetic horror: the others in the ring grinned. The scorpion's tail cracked down, time after time, till it sprawled dead in the center of the dying ring of fire. Douglas looked once more at Leech's face and read the satisfaction on it as Masters spoke.

"Get back to work."

As the men drifted away to their tasks, Leech kicked out the flames and ground the dead scorpion into the ground, covering it with sand. Masters ignored the incident and asked his second-in-command:

"Signed on your crew?"

"Yes."

"How many are you taking?"

"Seven's enough. Any more would get in the way. Seven's my lucky number."

Douglas spoke for the first time since coming out from Masters' office. It was his first bid to assert his position: it had to come, and now was as good a time as any.

"Eight is what you've got—I believe I'm in charge."

Leech ignored him, turning instead to Masters.

"Is our friend serious?"

Masters' reply was as smooth and gentle as oil.

"He will, of course, work very closely with you."

Realizing that they would be the only two officers on a long and dangerous mission, Douglas made his own effort at conciliation.

"Naturally I shall be grateful for any help I can get."

Leech turned to him:

"I see. Well, I've got a better idea. Let's keep it at seven—you go, I stay, then everybody's happy."

Seeing the danger, realizing that Leech meant what he said, Masters thrust his words between them, civilized clothing to hide Leech's naked aggression. He addressed himself to Douglas.

"I've asked Stores to kit you out. They'll be waiting for you. We'll talk more at dinner."

Douglas accepted the proffered shield for that moment. He realized that he was being got rid of so that Masters could talk to Leech, but as Masters was not coming on the trip, any influence he had with Leech would be temporary, and Douglas doubted whether even in camp it amounted to very much.

"Very well, sir." He started to salute, but checked himself. Instead he turned to Leech. "I'll want a full inspection at seven o'clock tomorrow morning, everything laid out, ready to load."

"Is there anything else you'd like?" Leech's words came flat and dangerous, but Douglas chose to not recognize the threat implicit in the tone of Leech's voice.

"No, that'll be all." Douglas smiled at Masters. "See you at dinner, sir."

Leech turned on Masters as Douglas strode away from them. He didn't raise his voice, but he looked dangerous.

"What does he mean?"

"Brigadier Blore's not too pleased with our record. He insists. We've got to take him."

Leech's voice grew harder, more menacing.

"I'll take him."

"And if he doesn't come back alive, we're out of business." The words came with quiet warning.

"*You're* out of business."

Masters spoke quickly, attempting to retrieve a situation he felt was slipping out of his control.

"You get well paid for these trips, don't forget."

"Oh, really."

Masters played his last card, the ace which had always won the vital trick in the past.

"I'll give you a bonus if you bring him back."

"How much?" The question came barefaced, unadorned by any attempt to hide the naked avarice.

"Dead: nothing; alive: two thousand pounds."

Leech's eyes narrowed as he considered the proposition. Then he laughed.

"You've just bought yourself an Englishman."

CHAPTER 5

THEIR EVENING MEAL OVER, Masters, Leech and Douglas sat together round a table in the café which served as the unit's headquarters. Round other tables sat most of the cosmopolitan crew who made up Masters' command. They played dominoes, drank and smoked with a shared air of self-reliance so extraordinary and complete that to the watching Douglas it seemed terrible, frightening. Masters was smoking a naguileh, Leech drinking whisky with controlled abandon.

One of the men playing dominoes suddenly laughed out loud, and Douglas looked at him, seeing him to be the finest as well as the most picturesque figure among the strange assortment in the café. He was a fine-boned, fine-featured Arab, with strikingly handsome features, large eyes and a trimmed black beard. He wore a burnous.

Douglas turned to Masters with unconcealed admiration.

"Where did you find him?"

"On one of my recruiting drives at Rabdah Prison. He's a Tunisian—Sadok." Masters smiled, almost with pride. "He threw a bomb into a café: a political crime; then he shot a policeman; a social crime; then, at his trial, he leaned over and punched the presiding officer on the nose: a personal crime. He got fourteen years. He's our demolition man."

Douglas' concern had evaporated a little after a good meal in the warm, exciting atmosphere of the café, but Masters' smooth catalogue of Sadok's crimes set him worrying again about the days, perhaps weeks which lay ahead in the company of Leech, Sadok, and others who might be even worse. Leech saw the expression on Douglas' face change, and showed his amusement. Masters missed it, intent on his summary. He nodded his head towards another man in his mid-thirties, dark, good-looking, tough, with a thick black moustache.

"Kostas Manou—Greek."

Masters paused, giving Douglas time to identify and take in the second man.

"Smuggler. He ran guns and explosives in and out of Egypt. They ran him in. I ran him out. He's in charge of armaments." Masters pointed again, this time with a lift of his chin. "Boudesh—Lebanese."

It took Douglas a moment or two to be sure whom Masters meant, for he had an instinctive inclination to think of all Lebanese as small dark men. Boudesh was big and fair, with a full face and massive shoulders. He looked as strong as an ox. Masters continued in the same didactic voice.

"Nice chap. Going with an Egyptian girl. Her brothers came to invite him to his own wedding. He shot them. Still a bachelor."

This time, Douglas kept his face under control, determined not to give Leech another opportunity to show his contempt. Had anyone but Masters been giving the descriptions, Douglas would not have believed them, or at best he would have treated the list of crimes as a wild exaggeration, but it didn't occur to him not to believe the colonel. Masters' calm, tutorial manner gave his words a horrible ring of truth. He touched Douglas on the arm and nodded again. Douglas followed Masters' eyes with a compulsive reluctance: he didn't want to see or hear any more, but knew he must.

"Kafkarides."

Douglas allowed his eyes to settle on the man picked out by Masters, and for the first time felt physically revolted without at once understanding why. Kafkarides was a lean compact figure, good looking in an almost English way, and he was laughing, his white, even teeth flashing in the bad light, his whole face animated and alive—except for the eyes. They were light in color, and flat and cold as a snake's. Douglas looked from Kafkarides to Leech as Masters continued speaking. The two men hadn't a feature in common, but emanating from both was the same aura of ruthless insanity.

". . . a Cypriot. His game was narcotics in a big way. Killed a couple of Egyptian customs men. In charge of transport and supplies. Those two," Masters gestured with a broad wave of his hand, "are Hassan and Assine. Senussi Arabs—guides."

Douglas looked away from Kafkarides to where the two Arabs sat together on the ground, their backs against a wall. They were sharing a pipe of keef and playing drums, breaking off frequently to smile into each other's face and fondle hands.

It was a scene of light relief and Douglas chuckled as he spoke to Masters, glad of the break provided by the two Senussi.

"Are they always so friendly?"

"All they need is keef and each other." Masters leaned back. "That's everybody."

The three officers sat looking at the men, and Douglas realized that those singled out by Masters were his complete command, with the exception of one—Leech.

"Aren't you going to tell him about me?"

43

Leech put his question aggressively, but without a shade of defiance, and Douglas felt that no revelation would invoke in Leech a sign of remorse or shame.

Masters looked faintly amused for the first time.

"You tell him."

"All right." Leech turned from Masters to Douglas, staring straight into his eyes. "Captain Leech—the black sheep of an otherwise admirable family, from County Dublin. Latest employment—master of a tramp steamer running around the Red Sea. Sank her for the insurance off Djibouti."

"He forgot to tell the crew." Masters interposed.

Leech continued as if the words were his and not Masters'. "They all drowned. All but one. He told the insurance company. I got fifteen years."

Masters rounded off Leech's recital. "When I met him at Rabdah Jail, he was king of it. They hated to see him go. But I needed him more than they did."

Douglas sat still in his chair, no longer making any attempt to conceal his disgust and apprehension. To command a group of killers was one thing, but to have as his fellow-officer, the man on whom he would have to rely for ninety per cent of the time, a cold-blooded wholesale murderer was something completely different.

Master read his face accurately.

"War is a criminal enterprise. I fight it with criminals."

Douglas' face didn't change. Masters' theories seemed too far removed from the standards of ordinary men to be worth consideration.

Realizing that he'd failed to reassure Douglas, Masters now injected a note of false optimism into his voice. "Not to worry. Leech knows the routine. He'll take you out and bring you back. Won't you Leech?"

Leech stood up, looking down at Douglas.

"If he's lucky."

Douglas watched him as, turning away, Leech strolled to the bar. He looked at Masters and asked the question that had been uppermost in his mind all evening.

"Will I be lucky?"

"It's up to you—and him, of course."

Douglas lay on his back in the bed they had provided for him, his eyes open, staring up into the blackness of the darkened room. He felt very much alone, and more than anything else he would have liked to be able to discuss the situation with someone of his own kind. Putting Leech and the rest of his cut-throat gang to one side, he was left only with Masters, a civilian like himself, but one who by design had managed to get himself into his present position. It was useless to appeal to Masters, for he was motivated only by a burning ambition to prove correct his theories on desert war. His catalogue of the men and his recital of the crimes and convictions which had brought them together in the Western Desert had been given without emotion. He saw the whole of his unit as expendable, and since Douglas had been wished on him by Higher Command, he was certainly of less value than the others, who had been carefully recruited, each for a specific purpose.

Douglas closed his eyes. There was nothing he could do but go through with it and hope for the best. He could expect no loyalty: he doubted whether any single member of the unit felt loyalty to anyone, and if they did, it would be extended to Leech who had already proved himself a natural leader. He remembered the two Senussi. They understood loyalty of a kind, but theirs was personal and closed, something they gave to each other and no one else. He tried to think of the members of the unit as individuals, instead of as a collection of cut-throats, but the picture in his mind remained much the same. He remembered what Masters had told him of the failed missions and of Leech's extraordinary ability to survive, and he found himself considering the possibility that Leech might be an enemy agent. From what he had learned of the Dubliner there was nothing in the other's makeup which led him to believe Leech would have any scruples about taking on such a role, provided always that there was more money in it than he could get from the British. The danger would be no greater, and might well be less than if he were acting only for the Allies.

He switched his thinking to Kafkarides, wondering for the second time why he saw a similarity between the Cypriot and Leech. He knew little of drug addicts, but he recognised that Kafkarides was one, and that he was bordering on insanity. Watching the Cypriot's behavior in the cafe had been sufficient to convince Douglas that Kafkarides was a law unto himself, and could only be swayed by a man he feared or from whom he could make a profit.

Douglas opened his eyes and looked fixedly into the darkness above his head. He could see nothing definable, anymore than he could see ahead into the days to come in the desert—with the German patrols the least of his worries.

CHAPTER 6

MAJOR WATKINS stepped on to the sand-packed parade ground of his camp near Cairo. Four three-ton trucks and two jeeps were drawn up in a straight line. In front of them stood their crews, rigidly at attention and, spread out in neat lines, the ammunition, stores, equipment and explosives needed for the expedition.

Captain Johnson, Watkins' second-in-command, strode forward to meet him. He halted in front of the major and saluted: reported the men, vehicles and equipment present and ready for inspection. Then, stepping smartly to the right, he fell in half a pace to the rear as Watkins moved forward to carry out the inspection.

Watkins was in no hurry, and he spent a long time on the inspection, devoting most of it to the examination of stores. He counted the boxes of detonators, and cutting a length of safety fuse he lit it and timed its burning. He overlooked nothing and, when he was at last satisfied, he turned to his second-in-command.

"Very good, Captain Johnson. Load all stores, prepare for departure in six hours. We cross the western checkpoint at first light tomorrow morning."

Watkins walked away as the order was given and the men fell to work. He was satisfied with the preparations and, as he had said to the brigadier the day before, he intended giving him a show. He knew how many times Masters' plans had miscarried, and he had no doubt in his mind why they had. You couldn't fight any type of war with cut-throat mercenaries, the sweepings of Middle East prisons, relying largely on loot, owing loyalty only to a paymaster. His own unit, the Long Range Desert Group, were picked men, each one a volunteer, but above all they were soldiers, trained to carry out orders without question. If Masters' lot hit trouble they would have got no more than they deserved, and they would be no loss to the British Army, of which they were not even members. He thought of Leech, comparing him with Johnson. Even Leech's captaincy was pseudo, a relic he had hung on to from the days when he had been master of a ship, before he'd sunk it with the crew aboard.

Watkins smiled to himself. He realized the dangers which lay ahead of the force he was taking behind the German lines. He knew the difficulties he would encounter and how heavy were the odds stacked against him. But the one thing he was not concerned about was the possibility that Masters' gang might beat him to it and succeed, before he got the chance, in blowing the petrol dump and cutting Rommel's lifeline to his Panzer Divisions, lying in wait west of Alamein.

Much farther to the west, and only twenty miles east and south of Alamein, the ragbag complex of Masters' headquarters, Douglas and the colonel paused before stepping down into the sand, looking towards where Leech and the rest of the men lounged around the single jeep and the two heavier trucks, already loaded. The MP's jeep which was to conduct them to the western checkpoint stood farther away, as if the military police were reluctant to be associated with the men, all of whom, like Douglas, were dressed in Italian uniforms.

Leech took a pace towards them as they approached: "Nice morning for a drive, Captain . . ."

Douglas looked at him, his face set. "I ordered an inspection at seven o'clock."

"I did it for you. All over—let's go."

Douglas ignored him; instead, he went to each truck and examined the contents, making a full circle of the vehicles. Masters and Leech followed him. Douglas' inspection was really a pretence and he knew it. With the stores already loaded and secured, his cursory examination was valueless. But if he couldn't stop Leech, he had at least to keep him in check: he couldn't allow him to override every order he gave. He had completed his tour of the vehicles and turned to Masters when Leech spoke.

"Find anything wrong?"

Douglas ignored him for the second time, and turned again to the colonel, but Leech was bent on provocation and climbed into the front of the jeep. Douglas, his lips tight, stepped up close to where Leech sat. He jerked his thumb savagely, indicating that Leech should sit in the back. Leech stared back at him and, behind Douglas, Masters glared at Leech. The three men remained still, a silent tableau, the rest of the unit watching them. Leech laughed suddenly and scrambled into the back of the jeep. Douglas saluted Masters and took the seat Leech had vacated next to the driver. It was a significant victory, and the first one he had chalked up. Masters waved his hand at the military police, and the small convoy moved off, his last words hanging over them like a blessing. "Good luck—keep in touch."

Douglas looked once at Colonel Masters as Kafkarides drove the jeep through the open gates. He stood, his hand still half raised; his lips pursed in speculation and his eyes distant and far-seeing; his mind four hundred miles away in Capris Magna. Douglas turned back to the dusty road, his thoughts still with Masters.

Was Masters as genuinely concerned as another officer of his rank would be at the prospect of striking a crippling blow at Rommel's supplies? Did he see the task of the mission for what it really was, a side swipe at the enemy which would make Montgomery's attack, when it came, a degree easier, limiting Rommel's maneuverability? Or was it so far as he was concerned, the be-all and end-all of the desert campaign, the justification of the theories he had propounded for so long?

Douglas grunted to himself and looked down at his map. Masters was as mad as the rest of his command. If Leech and the remainder were psychopaths and schizophrenics, Masters was paranoiac. He wondered what the others were like, the men higher up who must have some sort of control over Masters. He had met only one other member of Special Forces—Attwood; and he could hardly be considered as typical of anything except his own particular breed of junior staff officer.

During his time in North Africa, Douglas had heard a great deal about the operations carried out by units under the command of Special Forces. The exploits of Popski's Private Army and the more regular forces in the Long Range Desert Group had been recounted over and over again, no doubt with embellishments, but he did know that it was generally recognized that Special Forces had destroyed more Axis aircraft on the ground in rear areas than had the RAF in aerial combat or bombing and strafing missions. Certainly, he had never known that any unit existed like the one he now commanded. Masters must have considerable pull somewhere, or else those with the power had decided that extraordinary circumstances required extraordinary measures, and extraordinary people to carry them out.

Douglas looked up from his map as they approached the check-point. Speculation was now valueless, he was committed to an enterprise, and, co-opted or not, as a commissioned officer he had no alternative to carrying out to the best of his ability the orders he had been given. He sighed quietly and thought of Ann.

The MPs' jeep pulled off the road and stopped and the corporal in charge jumped from his seat and came over to where Kafkarides had pulled up, just short of the barrier. He saluted Douglas.

"This is as far as we can go, sir. The Germans have a few patrols going south of here."

Douglas returned his salute. "Thank you, corporal." The barrier swung up, and they moved forward into the Western Desert.

They drove fast for hours, the only sound apart from the sustained roar of the engines and the swish of their tires in the sand being the cracked laugh which came at intervals from Kafkarides. Douglas glanced at the Cypriot; at his permanently drawn back lips, showing his good teeth and red gums in a fixed grin; and at his bright, drugged eyes staring into the glare of the sun and the harsh reflection of it from the desert floor. He looked over his shoulder at the two trucks lumbering behind, piled high with stores, sand-tracks strapped to their sides. Sadok drove one of them, Hassan and Assine perched high behind him. Boudesh drove the wireless truck, his only passenger, Kostas Manou, dark, still and dangerous at his side. For the desert, the going was good, for they were still on the packed, small-pebbled floor of the northern part, stretching down from the Mediterranean. The Qattara, the dunes of the great Sand Sea and the Stone Desert would come later.

Douglas turned back and spotted where the track forked ahead of them, and he looked down at his map. He touched Kafkarides on the arm and shouted above the roar of the engine.

"Right—we go right," and he chopped with his hand at the right hand track. The Cypriot turned to him, laughing and nodding his head, but Douglas failed to see his quick glance at Leech or Leech's jerked thumb to the left. He was unprepared for the sudden swing to the south and was almost thrown out of the side of the jeep. He righted himself and leaning across in front of the Cypriot he switched off the ignition. The jeep slowed and came to a standstill, and when Douglas spoke he kept his voice deliberately low, putting into it a cutting edge.

"I said we go *right*."

Kafkarides stared at him, still grinning, then looked over his shoulder at Leech. As Douglas started to turn, he felt the map snatched away from him. Leech thrust it forward in his left hand, almost under Douglas' nose, while he stabbed at it with the forefinger of his right.

"That road was mined by the Italians a week ago." He paused, "It isn't all on the map, you know." He half threw the map back into Douglas' lap. "Try to stay lucky."

There was nothing Douglas could say, and he sat still and thoughtful as the laughing Kafkarides switched on the engine and continued down the left fork. He was going to have to leave a great deal to Leech. Ignorance of conditions and enemy activity in the area gave him no alternative. Well, so be it, but at the right time he intended to take command and push the operation through to a successful conclusion if it were humanly possibly. Till then he would rely on two things: Leech's knowledge and undoubted ability in certain spheres, plus something of which he was almost certain. For all the aura of insanity and violence which surrounded their every action, Leech and his crew of cut-throats were at heart survivors—he could only hope that a circumstance would not arise in which the sacrifice of himself would help them towards their end. He wondered what had happened to the other three British officers.

Late in the afternoon, the country began to break up, and Douglas had to turn more often to his map to be sure where they were. He did this solely for his own satisfaction, for Leech and the rest of the crew seemed in no doubt. A hour before darkness closed in, Leech tapped Kafkarides on the shoulder and pointed to an area lying to one side of the road and sheltered by a semi-circle of high mounds. Kafkarides swung off and headed towards it, the trucks closed behind him. Douglas sat silent, making no attempt to interfere or question Leech's order, and when Leech stood up, his arm raised above his head in a signal to stop, and they had slowed to a standstill, he climbed out and stood quietly by the jeep, watching. Under normal circumstances, he would have seen it as his duty to organize the camp for the night and personally see to the dozen and one things which were necessary, but he suspected that every man in the unit knew far better than he exactly what had to be done. He watched them for several minutes as they worked busily and fast at what to them was a well-known routine. They were good—he admitted it to himself with only a degree of reluctance. His eyes followed Kafkarides as he moved from vehicle to vehicle, checking engines and tires; mad or not, Kafkarides was a brilliant driver and seemed to know what he was up to.

Douglas shrugged—there was nothing for him to do. He walked away from the scene and sat down with his back against a rock. Lighting a cigarette, he pulled his portable chess set from his pocket and looked down at the pieces pegged in position, half way through the game he was playing with himself. He thought for a minute, then made his first move.

He had made only three or four moves when the failing light and an inability to concentrate made him fold the chess board and put it back in his pocket. He looked around him and was surprised at what had been done in such a short time. Every vehicle had been drawn into the cover of some mound or feature, camouflaged nets had been pegged out over them, bivouacs erected, and over a small fire Kafkarides and Kostas Manou were cooking a meal. Leech was speaking to Hassan and Assine, and the pair stood side by side holding hands, their heads cocked, listening intently, their eyes fixed on Leech. As he finished speaking, they melted away into the darkness, their hands still clasped.

Leech watched them go, and stood for a full minute after they had disappeared, staring into the night. He turned and strolled to where Boudesh sought a tuning signal on his radio. Reaching in front of the Lebanese, he picked up a sheet of paper and read through the transmission timings and the wavelengths to be used. He glanced at his watch and then stood without saying a word, observing Boudesh tuning in.

From where he sat in the shadow of the rock, Douglas could see Leech plainly, silhouetted against the glow of the fire, his face clear in the light from the moon. There was something about the Irishman which simultaneously attracted and repelled, and Douglas found himself thinking hard to find a parallel, without getting beyond the jungle and the zoo and the most savage of their occupants. Leech's face was expressionless as he watched Boudesh at the controls of the radio, and from his vantage point Douglas studied the strong face with its powerful jaw, the hooked nose jutting arrogantly from under the thick brows. He realized suddenly that Leech was a fine looking man, impressive, and he wondered where the mercenary had first gone wrong, what had started him on the road leading to cold-blooded, wholesale murder, and a disregard—more than that—a deep-rooted contempt for social laws and accepted principles of behavior.

Leech moved suddenly, leaning forward to listen to a brief aside from the Lebanese, his body as tense as a coiled spring. Douglas looked at the two figures. He hadn't realized before how big and powerful Leech was, and he wondered how it was possible for him to have missed something so obvious as the athlete's physique he couldn't help but admire from where he sat. He cast his mind back to their first meeting in the café, and the antipathy Leech had aroused in him. That was the answer to it, he supposed: he'd put Leech down as a braggart; he'd expected him to swagger and strut, and when he hadn't and his face had remained always expressionless—only the eyes and occasionally the lips augmenting what he said— Douglas had concentrated on his words and the tone he used when he spoke.

Douglas shrugged mentally at how much he had missed, but he felt that, almost certainly, in the final analysis, Leech was still a butcher and, if half of what he suspected was true, a treacherous butcher into the bargain.

A sharp whistle broke the train of his thought, and Douglas swung his eyes from Leech to the camp fire. Kafkarides was holding out a mess tin with one hand and miming eating with the other, finishing up with a beckoning gesture. Kafkarides' eyes shone brighter than ever and his fixed grin gleamed white behind the dancing flames. Douglas chose the line he was to take, and called out:

"Thank you very much. Bring it over here would you?"

Kafkarides didn't move at once. In the light from the

fire, Douglas saw his eyes swing to the wireless truck, and he saw Leech look up and, after a pause, nod his head. Kafkarides got to his feet at once, rising easily from his cross-legged position behind the fire. He came across to where Douglas sat, and handed him the mess tin of food, his grin less fixed and his eyes more calculating. Douglas took the proffered food with a smile.

"Thank you very much," he said, and watched Kafkarides slip back a pace or two before turning and going back to the others. He had only taken the first mouthful of food when he half sensed, half glimpsed a figure materialize at his side. He looked up and saw Leech staring down at him. He paused, his fork half way to his mouth, and he spoke with a trace of humor, something brought about by his observation of Leech when he had stood at the wireless truck, his only concern the business in hand.

"It's a pity you don't play chess."

If he'd hoped for a conciliatory response from Leech, he didn't get it.

"If you want to wait somewhere, I'll pick you up on the way back."

Douglas smiled, adapting himself to Leech's mood, a mood which at least had the merit of being always consistent: Leech made bald statements. Even if he never explained what motivated them, he meant exactly what he said.

"It sounds delightful. Why?"

"I can manage without you."

"I'm staying right with you, Captain Leech."

Leech looked down at Douglas without a trace of expression, weighing him up against what he remembered of the other British officers he had taken out into the desert and failed to bring back alive. When he spoke, it was the very ordinariness of his tone which added to the menace of his words.

"Just don't get in my way."

Douglas played it far cooler than he felt, speaking deliberately in a voice he would have used to a temperamental, high-strung woman. "Get some sleep, you'll feel better."

"I don't sleep—very much."

Already committed to a line, Douglas had no alternative but to continue with it.

"Then you can keep an eye on the sentries—I'm going to turn in."

"You do just that."

Leech turned quickly and moved away to the fire and the food that was awaiting him: Douglas felt behind him for a blanket from his bedroll and pulled it round his shoulders. Night air in the desert always struck cold, but the chill inside him had nothing to do with the temperature.

He started to rethink the position he was in: the position to which his own decision had brought him. He had decided at one stage to have no part of the operation, and his decision had been based on his knowledge of the firm agreement made by British Petroleum with the British Army. He had been seconded on one assurance, that he would be employed only in base areas, and that assurance in itself excused him from employment in the kind of role in which he was now engaged. He sucked at his teeth and sighed. Vanity! He had nothing else to blame but just that. The idea of Leech chortling over his decision to withdraw had been the intellectual straw which had broken his considered intention to oppose Brigadier Hommerton's veiled threat. He was reasonably sure that the army would not have risked a court-martial in view of the written agreement between itself and the British Petroleum Company.

He reached up to his breast pocket for a handkerchief, and his fingers checked for a moment at the unfamiliar touch of the Italian buttons. Italian! What a fool! No officer or soldier could be made to wear the uniform of the enemy, for in the event of capture it meant only one thing—court-martial and death by firing squad. He sat with his hand still fingering the button, wondering how it had been possible for him to have missed something so obvious. He started to think back to the suggestion by Masters that they should wear the uniform of the lesser half of the European Axis, and the arguments he had advanced in favor of them doing so. Masters' contention had been that from experience he knew that the German's contempt for their allies was so great that if they met an Italian patrol in the desert they ignored it completely. It was safer to be Italian than to be British if the Germans were encountered. He had been so swayed by the logic of Masters' reasoning that he had not considered the one point which really mattered and was covered by the Geneva Convention. His shoulders sagged under the blanket, and then he found himself laughing, for if he chose he could return at once to base and no one could do anything about it—but he also knew that this was something he could not bring himself to do.

He pulled the blanket closer round his body and lay back in the sand. For good or ill, he was committed: he couldn't see any alternative to seeing the job through and taking responsibility for its eventual success or failure.

CHAPTER 7

THE FOLLOWING MORNING they continued on across the Qattara Depression, the sun beating down on their heads, the metal of the vehicles growing too hot to touch. The salt flats over which they drove were baked and cracked after the long summer, now drawing to its close but not yet over. Douglas sat the drive out in silence as Kafkarides hurtled the jeep across the sweltering bed of the Depression, his eyes moving constantly from the broken undulating landscape ahead of him to his map, and from the map to his compass.

Somewhere ahead of them was an oasis, and Douglas reckoned they were four or five miles short of it, and so was unprepared when Leech suddenly stood up in the swaying vehicle and signalled the convoy to a halt. As they ground to a standstill, Douglas looked up to where Leech stood, and asked sharply, "What is it?"

"Waterhole—let's take a look." Leech jumped down and waving to the two Senussi guides to follow him he set out for a low hill to the side of the one which lay in front of them. Douglas joined him, and they labored up the slope together, Douglas wondering how the hell Leech had managed to recognize a particular hill which seemed in no way different from a thousand others. Near the top, they went more cautiously, till at last they were looking down on the few scattered palms surrounding a small oasis. Arabs and camels moved about near the waterhole. Leech looked at them through his binoculars, which then, without speaking, he passed to Hassan. The Senussi looked through them quickly and spoke one word.

"Barvssi."

Leech thought about it for a moment before taking the glasses and looking again.

"What does that mean?" Douglas asked.

"The Barvssi could be dangerous. It depends on who's paying them." Leech handed the glasses to Douglas. Looking through them, he counted quickly and made his observation.

"Six men, six camels."

Leech asked quickly, "No lead camel?"

Douglas shook his head and Leech turned at once to Hassan and Assine.

"Why is there no lead camel?"

Douglas followed the Arabic with difficulty.

"More men, more camels following, maybe now, maybe later."

Leech considered what Hassan had said for only a second.

"You go round the back and see if you can see the others."

Hassan turned at once, touched hands with Assine, and was gone. Leech spoke to Douglas, preoccupied with the development, his tone level and unprovocative.

"This is an advance party, the rest could arrive any minute. He's gone to spot them."

"But we've got to have water."

"Exactly."

Douglas thought for a moment before making his suggestion.

"We're Italians aren't we—why don't we go and trade?"

"Are you asking me or telling me?" The question came from Leech with a hard humor.

"I'm asking you."

Leech laughed, and this time there was genuine humor in the sound. Douglas and Assine at his heels, he scrambled fast down the side of the hill to where the rest of the unit were waiting. As he reached the men, he called out to them.

"There's an advance party of Barvssi at the oasis. We're an Italian patrol who need food and water—let's go to market." And over his shoulder to Assine, "You go ahead and tell them the story." He called again to the others as he climbed into the jeep. "Everybody else —parl' Italiano."

Douglas jumped into his seat, thankful that his Italian was bound to be better than that of the Barvssi. Leech reached over to the radio, switched it on and sought the station he wanted, and the convoy drove confidently towards the oasis to the sound of Rossini. Douglas glanced once at Leech before they got there: there was a deliberate expression of pain on Leech's face at the sound of the opera, but his eyes moved quickly over the group of Arabs as the jeep drew near to them.

The Arabs were friendly and obviously pro-Italian: they were smiling and waving before the convoy had come to a halt.

Douglas spoke from the corner of his mouth.

"It looks as if we chose the right side."

Leech grunted. "Don't be so sure. If they offer you tea—drink it. If they offer you food—eat it."

Douglas left the talking to Leech, and within minutes they were both seated on the ground, their backs to the jeep, the Arabs facing them in a semi-circle. Kafkarides started to top up the radiators of the vehicles, while the remaining four men filled jerrycans from the waterhole.

Most of the formalities were over, and Douglas

watched the tea being poured, accepted it, and tried to keep the nausea from his face as he sipped at the treacly, peppermint-flavored drink. He took the sweetmeats when they were offered and passed them to Leech. The tea, the sickly food, and the afternoon sun made him feel hot and uncomfortable, and he pulled the silk square free from his throat.

Leech popped one of the sweetmeats into his mouth without looking down, his eyes catching the arrested look on one of the Arab's faces. He saw him nudge the man next to him, very gently. Leech pushed his field-cap to the back of his head, the movement covering the swift jerk of his eyes as he followed the Arab's stare. At once he was smiling and leaning forward as he addressed the Arab leader.

"Music?"

The Arab nodded, grinning back at him, and Leech rose to his feet. He reached into the jeep and switched on the radio, every movement casual and unconcerned, except the last.

He turned back from the jeep in a single fast, swivelling movement, and Douglas spotted the cradled sub-machine gun in his hands in the second before Leech opened fire inches from his head. The bullets blasted into the Arabs, bowling three of them over where they sat; the other three were on their feet and running before the first three had fallen back into the sand. Raising his head from where he had thrown himself, Douglas saw Leech raise his gun and fire again, and heard another gun open up from behind the jeep. The running Arabs were cut down within ten yards of where they had sat.

Douglas got to his feet, his face white, muscular control nearly gone, his hands and legs trembling with shock at the unexpected, murderous attack. He opened his mouth to speak, but his words were drowned in the sudden renewed firing as Leech and Kafkarides poured burst after burst into the bodies of the fallen men. At last there was silence, and Douglas was able to tear his eyes away from where the jumping bodies relapsed into a blood-soaked stillness, and turn them on Leech, standing with the gun still cradled in his hands, his face blank, the lips turned down slightly at the corners.

When he spoke, he heard in the unsteady note of his own voice the horrified incredulity that he felt.

"What—what did you do that for?" He felt the inadequacy of the words even as he uttered them.

"I didn't like the teal" Leech spat the words at him before turning to the others and shouting out to them, "See if there's anything we need in the packs."

Leech didn't move from where he was standing, but watched the others as they ran forward to ransack the baggage of the Arabs. Douglas had regained most of his equilibrium, and he took a pace towards Leech, his face still pale, but no longer with shock: it was drained by the seething anger which filled him at the senseless murder of the six Arabs.

"You must be out of your mind—if anybody's going to be killed, *I* give the order—is that clear?"

Leech took the two paces necessary to close the gap between them. He ground out his reply, his teeth clenched and his lips barely moving.

"Somebody gave the show away."

Douglas blinked, his mind fighting to think rationally. His fury hadn't permitted him to think that there might be a reason for Leech's action.

"Who?"

"You!" Leech reached up and ripped the British identity discs from where they hung from Douglas' neck, exposed by the removal of his scarf. He threw them into the sand, and his next words bit into

Douglas. "If you'd stayed at home, they'd still be alive!"

Douglas' reply was almost a whisper, and it was addressed more to himself than to Leech. "I'm staying." He turned and looked at the bodies, taking in the bright life-blood staining the white robes of the dead Arabs; his stomach sick with the consciousness of his own guilt: if he'd not been so preoccupied with the shortcomings of Leech and the rest of his gang, he might have been less careless, giving more thought to the part he was to play and less to conjecture about the future behavior of the others.

Kostas Manou came up to where the two men stood, Douglas trying hard to find words acceptable to himself which would at the same time express his regret that his carelessness had contributed to the death of the Arabs; he still couldn't accept that their killing had been unavoidable. The arrival of the Greek was the key which served to disengage the locked eyes of the two men. They turned to him, Leech examining the radio set Kostas Manou carried in his arms.

"German. Every patrol in the south would have been on to us five hours after we left them."

It was the key brick in the arch of evidence. Douglas was prepared to make his admission without reservations, but before he had the chance the running figure of Hassan appeared, and they all waited for the Senussi to come up to where they stood.

Hassan spoke to Leech in Arabic so fast that Douglas couldn't follow what he said. When the Arab finished speaking, Leech turned to Douglas.

"There are about fifty more. They'll be here in four hours."

He turned and walked towards the jeep, Douglas following him. Leech picked up the map and studied it.

"We can't go that way."

"Well, we're not going back." Douglas spoke quickly, perhaps too quickly, attempting to forestall something which might not be said.

"Then there's only one other way we can go."

They turned together and looked at the solid cliff which marked the western limit of the Qattara Depression. Standing shoulder to shoulder, they were apparently united for the first time.

"Is there a pass?"

Leech shook his head. "Not for one hundred and twenty miles, right down at Siouwa."

"Let's have a look."

They drove on across the baked salt flats, to the eye hard and strong enough to carry their transport, but capable, even after the long, hot summer, of collapsing and swallowing heavy armored vehicles. They arrived at the foot of the cliffs and got out. They stared up at the sharp-angled face and Leech shook his head.

"We'll have to go back."

Douglas barely glanced at him as he studied the broken face of the cliffs. The problem had ceased to present itself to him as a military one, or even as something personal between himself and Leech. It had become an engineering problem—and he was an engineer. His mind worked quickly, seeking a solution, his memory going back to his cursory inspection of the already loaded vehicles. There had been a drum of cable in the back of each of the two bigger trucks. He strode over to one of them and uncovered a drum. He turned to Leech, the authority of professionalism and knowledge in his voice.

"How long are these cables?"

"About two hundred and fifty feet each." Leech looked from the exposed cable up to the top of the cliff, and back to Douglas. "It'll never work." But Douglas wasn't listening; he was already unbuttoning his jacket. Throwing it down, he turned to Kostas Manou.

"Is there any string?"

The Greek nodded slowly. "Yes—yes, there's string."

"Well, get it." Douglas strode to the base of the cliff, then along it, his head raised, studying the lie of its broken face. Nearly a hundred yards from where he'd started, he stopped, looking up a section of the cliff where the face was less sharply angled over a ten or twelve foot width. He looked back towards the trucks and saw Kostas Manou coming towards him, a large ball of thick string in his hands. He waited for the Greek to arrive and, when he did, took the string from him, handing back the loose end and throwing the ball to the ground so that the string ran freely away from it. He pointed to the top of the cliff and nodded. Kostas Manou looked into Douglas' eyes, lack of comprehension obvious in his own, but in them also an intelligent appreciation that Douglas was aware of what he was doing. He thrust the loose end of string in his mouth and set off up the cliff face, rarely erect, often crouched forward like an ape, and sometimes using hands and feet when the angle became sharper and the going harder. Douglas stayed where he was, paying out and measuring the string. At last, Kostas Manou was at the top, standing upright and looking down at Douglas.

Douglas doubled the figure he had measured, and spoke aloud, but to himself. "Three hundred and twenty-seven feet. We might even have a bit to spare." He turned to the nearest man in the loose group that had assembled behind him: it was Kafkarides, his face unchanged, his grin still fixed, his eyes cold, bright, incomprehensible.

"Shackle those two cables together." He turned to Boudesh, "Are you strong?" The Lebanese nodded, and grunted with pleasure: his expertise with wireless, a trade he had learned and developed, was unimportant to him; recognition of his physical strength, for which he could claim little if any credit, mattered to him.

"Then get the end of that cable to the top of the cliff." Douglas turned to Leech who was standing behind him. "Coming up?"

Leech shook his head slowly. "No, I'll stay here."

Douglas turned to Kostas Manou, who had arrived back, hot and panting.

"Stakes, hammer, blocks and pulleys."

The Greek moved away to collect the gear, comprehension slowly dawning in his intelligent eyes. Douglas turned to the others, pointing at the stores truck. "Unload that truck—let's get going."

Leech watched from below as, with Boudesh in the lead, and Sadok and Kafkarides strung at intervals behind him, the cable was carried slowly up the cliff face. He looked at the chain thrown round the rock outcrop at the foot of the cliff, at the pulley attachment and the cable passing through it, and then at the unloaded stores truck. Perhaps—but the odds were against it.

Douglas and Kostas Manou worked together at the top of the cliff, anchoring the other block and pulley. When they'd finished they stood together, waiting for Boudesh as he labored up the last and sharpest part of the incline. Douglas looked at the Greek's face, shining with sweat, his eyes eager.

"You've done this before, haven't you?"

Kostas Manou grinned. "With guns—yes. With trucks—no."

They took the end of the cable from Boudesh as he reached them, and passed it through the pulley. Douglas handed the end of it to Kostas Manou.

"Take this down—shackle it to the back of the unloaded stores-truck."

"Yes, Captain. Is it going to work?"

Douglas looked down the cliff face to where Leech lounged against one of the vehicles, an arm resting on the hood.

"It's got to."

Kostas Manou scrambled down to Leech and the trucks, the cable running freely through the pulley above him. He shackled it to the back of the empty truck. Sadok was in the driving seat of the wireless truck, Kafkarides behind the wheel of the jeep, the two vehicles joined by a towing wire, and the other end of the cable shackled to the back of the wireless truck.

Leech called out to the two drivers, involving himself a little in the operation.

"Start your engines."

They started up and looked back over their shoulders, Sadok impassive, Kafkarides showing his cynicism. Hassan and Assine stood well clear, clasping each other's hands, their faces concerned, worried because they didn't understand what was happening. Kostas Manou, his face alive with interest and optimism, looked up to where Douglas and Boudesh stood at the top of the cliff.

Douglas waved to the group below, and the truck and the jeep moved forward, first taking up the slack of the tow-wire between them. The cable lifted between the two pulleys as Sadok and Kafkarides drove slowly forward away from the cliff face, and then it was tightening between the back of the stores-truck and the top pulley; raised clear of the rock and shale, the cable sang as it took the strain. The truck moved backwards over the last few level yards and started its ascent up the shelving face of the cliff.

Douglas crossed his fingers and glanced at Boudesh. The big Lebanese revealed nothing of what was going on in his mind: he stood quite still, his powerful body as rough-hewn as the rocks around him, and Douglas turned his eyes back to the slow-turning wheels of the empty truck. It came on steadily, with hardly a check, till at last it was crawling over the final, sharpest-angled few yards of the slope. Then he was standing to one side as it came past him, and signalling to Sadok and Kafkarides to stop. Douglas jerked his head at Boudesh, and the pair of them worked together unshackling the cable from the back of the truck.

"Take it down—we'll have the jeep next."

The Lebanese set off down the slope, and Douglas climbed into the driving seat of the truck and drove it clear of the cliff edge. Below, on the desert floor, Assine and Hassan threw their arms round each other and danced happily in the sand; Sadok smiled as he unfastened the tow-wire; and Kafkarides' fixed grin grew wider, and his mad eyes brighter still.

The lighter jeep went up easily, and watching it, Douglas' stomach muscles relaxed. From where he stood, he could detect the new mood of the men in their quicker more confident movements. He shouted down to Leech: "Unload the truck." And he called to Sadok and Kafkarides to come to the top.

They joined the empty stores-truck and the jeep with a towline. It was going to be a straight pull for the last vehicle, with only the angle of the cable running off the top pulley to break the dead drag, but Douglas was no longer worried, the first two vehicles had come up easier than he had thought they would. He had watched the cable and the movement of the stores-truck and the jeep with a professional eye, gauging strain and drag as an engineer. He walked to the crest of a low, hard-packed dune, throwing down his mapcase and pulling his field-glasses free from his neck: he lay down, and before giving his attention to the new, drifting terrain of the Sand Sea, he looked over his shoulder at Boudesh, standing feet astride, the angle of his head showing his absorption in the scene in the Depression. In the moment before he shouted, Douglas found himself thinking of the Colossus at Rhodes viewing the ancient ships of the Mediterranean as they sailed between its bestriding legs.

"OK—let it come when they're ready."

He turned back to the desert, but for a minute or two his eyes were turned inwards, seeing nothing of the scene in front of him. He felt a new confidence; his professionalism was paying off; Leech was out of his depth and forced to stand aside while Douglas took over the command that had been contested even before they set off.

Leech, Kostas Manou, Assine and Hassan stood round the last truck, their heads turned towards the top of the cliff, watching Boudesh. He waved to them and then shouted down, his words faint but carrying clearly through the still desert air.

"*He* says—when you are ready."

Leech swung his arm from waist high behind him to shoulder height in front of him, a gesture as plain as the words he shouted up to Boudesh. "Take it away!"

Kostas Manou looked down at the still loaded truck: raised his eyes till they met Leech's, his even stare supporting the accusation in his voice.

"*He*—says unload."

Leech looking uncomfortable was something which neither Kostas Manou nor the two Arabs had seen before. The general, embracing orders covering objectives given by Masters were one thing: a specific order given by Douglas was something entirely different. He made no reply, but signalled again to Boudesh at the top of the cliff face. The watchers below saw the Lebanese turn away from them and make an overarm, thrusting gesture at where Sadok and Kafkarides sat waiting in their vehicles. Within seconds, the cable moved as the slack was taken up, till it ran out as tight as a fiddler's string from the back of the wireless truck to the single pulley anchored out of sight over the brink of the cliff. Leech and the two Senussi were standing in front of the hood, on the desert side of the truck, Kostas Manou at the back of it, where he'd shackled the cable. The truck started to move towards him, and for a second he stood his ground as if by standing between the truck and the slope he could prevent the stupidity of Leech's pride threatening the clear success of Douglas' plan. He met Leech's level stare and the fresh-fused defiance which had begun to burn in him spluttered and died. He had taken orders from Leech for too long. He lowered his eyes and stepped aside as the back of the truck moved towards him.

Kafkarides, at the wheel of the jeep, edged it forward, feeling first the tug of the truck behind, then a slackening and a released surge as Sadok's truck took the weight of the other and overcame it. Kafkarides played his throttle, directing the power of the jeep only to assisting Sadok as the bigger vehicle tugged at the near dead weight of the wireless truck in the Depression: he was helping Sadok, not attempting to drag him faster than the revolutions of the Arab's engine. The wheels of the two vehicles spat sand, gripped deeper, and holding their grip, moved forward. Douglas studied the lie of the land: it looked difficult and dangerous. He took a compass bearing, allowed for the magnetic variation, and marked a chinagraph line on his map. Pinpointing his position and the line of the route he intended to follow was one thing, but maintaining direction through the drifting Sand Sea with its ever changing dunes was going to be something quite different. His thinking was broken into by the suddenly increased roar from the engines of the two vehicles behind and below him. He turned quickly and looked down at them: they were barely moving, the cable straining and singing its protest. Douglas scrambled to his feet as they stopped altogether, their rear wheels beginning to sink in the sand. They strained for seconds while he watched, Sadok's and Kafkarides' faces set and tense, and then they were creeping forward again, very slowly, making inches at a time.

Douglas lifted his eyes to the cliff edge where Boudesh leaned forward, gazing down at the wireless truck coming up. He shouted, "Boudesh!" And the Lebanese turned slowly and looked at him across the fifty yards which separated them. "Is that truck loaded?" Boudesh didn't reply; holding Douglas' eyes for seconds only, he turned again and looked down the slope.

Douglas slid down the side of the low dune and started to run towards the Lebanese. He cleared the taut cable like a hurdler, slowed down at the last moment, and halted alongside Boudesh, his eyes fixed on the fully loaded wireless truck grinding laboriously up towards him. One of its rear wheels struck a rock only a little larger than the others and it stopped. Douglas dropped his eyes to the cable, listening as the straining steel wires took on a new note. He felt the sweat break out on his forehead and trickle coldly down his face; his stomach muscles bunched, and his hands began to tremble. He was helpless, unable to do anything but hope and pray. He was trapped by Leech's failure to comply with an order clearly given. He couldn't order Sadok and Kafkarides to stop and back towards the edge of the cliff, for the wireless truck would then be going forward and the front wheels would be turned by any obstruction: it would go off the best path and turn over within yards, and if it really got going it would drag the other two trucks over the edge after it.

He watched the cable, and saw the first thin wire part and curl back, and then another and another. He shouted his warning to the men at the foot of the cliff. "The cable's going!" And he threw himself sideways as the final strands snapped and one end of the cable snaked back between him and Boudesh, missing them by inches. From where he had thrown himself he watched the wireless truck run back down the slope, gathering speed. The front wheels hit something and twisted. The truck checked and then went over. It rolled and leaped down the cliff, bouncing off the outcrops of rock, its contents flung in all directions and falling like giant hail through the air.

Hassan and Assine ran like frightened wraiths out into the desert, their hands still clasped. Kostas Manou moved quickly out of danger and stood watching from one side. Leech moved, reluctantly, and not as far away as the others, and when what was left of the truck came to rest it was only yards from where he stood.

Douglas scrambled down the cliff face, and ran across to where the wrecked truck lay on its side. Leech was standing on the far side of it. Douglas' anger had kept him at a flat run till he was almost up to the truck, and he had to put out his hands to check himself. He stood for half a minute, his chest heaving and his mouth open, glaring at Leech over the wreckage. Leech was the first to speak.

"The radio's gone. No more music."

"I ordered you to unload." Douglas' voice was a flat challenge.

"Yes." Just that. Nothing else. It wasn't even a question—merely agreement.

Douglas turned to the others, finding it impossible to handle Leech: there were some kind of rules which governed any situation—Leech recognized none.

"Salvage what you can from this. We spend the night at the top of the cliff." The men looked from him to Leech. Douglas spoke again. "Let's get moving." They moved off at once and started on the job of salvage.

By dusk, camp had been made, the vehicles camouflaged, and the last of the stores carried to the cliff top. The men with the exception of Boudesh were round the fire where a meal was being cooked. Douglas sat alone, the portable chess set open in front of him. Leech stood to one side of Boudesh, watching him as he worked at the smashed wireless set, completely absorbed in his task.

Only a few miles to the east, Major Watkins and his convoy pulled into the oasis which Douglas and his men had quit earlier in the day. Watkins climbed out of his jeep, his face set and his mind already made up. He had spotted the bodies of the dead Arabs minutes before he braked the jeep and waited for the rest of the convoy to drive in behind him. He walked slowly between the scattered palms round the waterhole, glancing down at each of the six blood-soaked bodies as he passed it. When his second-in-command joined him, he spoke.

"Those bloody butchers."

Johnson looked quickly at his CO, gauging his mood. He remembered Watkins doing quite a bit of butchering in his time.

"Masters' mob?"

"Who else? Now every Arab for two hundred miles will know that there are British patrols in the Qattara Depression."

Johnson wondered whether Watkins' main concern was for the Arabs, or for the fact that their own unit was now endangered by an action of the mercenaries.

"Do you think that we should change course, sir?"

"Impossible. This is the only track through the Qattara. We have to carry on to the south till we reach the pass."

"Yes, sir." Johnson waited for the next order.

"Get some of the men to throw sand over these corpses, would you—they're beginning to stink."

Johnson turned and repeated the order to the WO standing five paces behind them.

Watkins looked to the west, where he could see the cliffs of the Depression.

"We'll camp here for the night, and move off before first light."

"Yes, sir."

Johnson saluted and walked away to make the necessary arrangements, glad that they were to have one night under the palms, near water. He glanced at the soldiers already at work, digging the shallow graves.

The Arab scout, thrown ahead of the main body, labored up the last hill south of the oasis, walking his camel behind him. He lay down just below the crest and edged upwards till he was peering down at the palms and the water below him. He picked out the

British soldiers, and, as he recognized the work they were at, his eyes narrowed. He counted swiftly, men and vehicles, and slid back well below the crest before mounting his camel and racing back to meet the main body of Barvssi coming up from Siouwa.

CHAPTER 8

It was just before dawn when the sound of engines drifted up from the floor of the Depression to where the unit lay sleeping near the cliff top. The three Arabs were the first to wake, and they slipped away silently to the cliff edge and peered down. Leech followed them, and one by one, the rest of the unit. Douglas was the last to be awakened by the sound, and he lay for a full minute, orientating himself, before throwing aside his blanket and joining the others.

At first, the watching men could see nothing, although their eyes were all turned in the direction from which the sound came, from their right, to the south, out of the wadi they had been following till Hassan had warned them of the approach of the main body of the Arabs. Douglas wondered whether the Arabs had made their way to the oasis during the night.

As it got lighter, the watchers on the cliff top picked out the leading vehicles of a convoy following the course of the wadi. It was a German convoy, and was made up of troop-carrying half-trucks and desert scout cars. Every vehicle was packed with men, and as they drew nearer Douglas could pick out the arms they carried and the machine guns mounted in the back of the trucks. He glanced quickly at the unit strung out along the top of the cliff to the right of him. Every face was intent, but on none of them was anything approaching apprehension: each man was interested, curious, and nothing more. He looked back to the bottom of the Depression and saw a section of the column pull off the track and conceal their vehicles behind the ridged mounds and small hillocks. They set up mortars and light machine guns, all aligned on the track running towards the oasis from which Douglas and the unit had come the afternoon before. He felt a sense of relief, realizing that the ambush being layed by the Germans was almost certainly intended to catch the men who watched with interest from above. They'd been lucky, but he found himself wondering how the Germans had got on to them. The front half of the convoy moved on farther up the track before pulling off and taking up positions largely aimed at the direction from which they had come. Douglas recognized the classic ambush, two halves with the open killing ground between.

The German troops worked very quickly and efficiently setting up their mortars and siting their machine guns; an officer walked over and examined the wrecked wireless truck lying on its side at the foot of the cliff. He looked suddenly up the broken face, and the men at the top froze till he shrugged and walked back to a commandpost at the top of a dune. From his vantage point, Douglas could see nearly every one of the German troops, but he realized that they were concealed from the view of any unit moving down the track from the oasis.

The faint sound of engines came again to the watching men, and Douglas looked for the second time to the south, failing to see anything. He frowned to himself but, even as he puzzled over his failure to pick out the vehicles whose engines he could hear, he noticed some of the unit looking to the left, to the opposite direction from the one he was searching. He turned and followed their eyes. Out of the dawn, their vehicles shimmering in the rays of the sun, another convoy approached from the direction of the oasis, driving fast. It consisted of a column of three-ton trucks, all with troops aboard, and two jeeps, one leading the convoy, and one bringing up the rear. They were British.

Douglas caught his breath. So certain that his own unit was the intended victim of the German ambush, he had not given a thought to the possibility that any other might be involved. He watched the leading jeep pass where the first German troops lay concealed, waiting to close the trap behind the rear vehicle of the British convoy. He lifted his right hip off the ground and, reaching down, pulled his pistol clear of its holster. He had half raised it to fire warning shots to the British convoy in the Depression when it was wrested from his hand, and before he could turn, a powerful forearm swept across the lower part of his face, forcing his chin up, and he felt the prick of a knife point at his throat and heard Leech's voice, quiet at his ear.

"We're in the petrol and pipeline business, remember, sir?"

Douglas tried once to free himself, but was helpless in Leech's grip, and as he cleared his mouth and opened it to shout he felt the point of the knife bite into the skin of his neck, and at once the warm trickle of blood as it ran down his throat. He watched helplessly as the rear jeep passed the drop-end of the ambush, and heard the signalling shot as the first German mortar bomb left its tube. Every German mortar and machine gun opened up simultaneously, the bombs landing with deadly accuracy among the British vehicles, and thousands of bullets from the Spandaus ripped into them as they zigzagged madly in an effort to escape the leaden death—but there was no escape. As Douglas watched, the trucks were knocked out one by one, some exploding in great sheets of flame as demolition charges were hit; others, with their drivers killed, lurched to a standstill or raced on till they smashed into the dunes and rocks around them. The Germans kept up their deadly fire, even on the stationary vehicles, till their petrol was ignited and they too burned. The leading jeep was the last to be hit. It raced round for what seemed an age, dodging in and out of the smashed and burning convoy, its light machine gun blazing away at the tops of the dunes. Then, a lucky mortar bomb must have made a direct hit on it, for in the midst of a frantic dash between two dunes it went up with a roar, turning over and over, throwing its occupants clear, so that they hung for a second in the air like cloth puppets before falling down on the desert beside their blazing jeep.

The German soldiers came down warily from their positions, ready for any trick. They moved about the burning vehicles, checking the bodies for any sign of life and where they found it they extinguished it rapidly and without fuss, with a single shot or the swift thrust of a bayonet.

Leech retained his grip on Douglas, the knife still held at his throat till the last German soldier had climbed back into the half-trucks and driven off. As they disappeared down the wadi in the direction from which they had come, Leech stood up and sheathed his knife, saying nothing, waiting for Douglas. The RE got slowly to his feet, his face white under his tan.

"You play dirty, Captain Leech."

"I play safe."

Leech turned his back on Douglas and waved to the waiting men, following them more slowly as they swarmed down the cliff face to the still burning convoy. Their faces were alight at the prospect of loot, and some of them wore a sated, contented look: from their privileged position of safety it had been as entertaining and inevitable as a bull-fight, as exciting as a Roman Circus.

Douglas went after them down the slope and when he reached the bottom, they had already fallen to their work. Hassan and Assine danced like chorus boys from body to body, strapping the dead British soldiers' watches on their forearms, going through their wallets with swift deft movements. When either of them made a particularly good find, he rushed to the other waving his capture, and for a few seconds they would stand quite still, their hands clasped, a look of rapture on their faces. Kafkarides and Boudesh searched the burned-out trucks for undamaged spare parts, spare wheels, anything that could be put to use. Kóstas Manou gathered up the Sten guns and LMGs. Sadok came away from the least damaged truck, a smiling look of delight on his face, and in his arms an intact box of explosive. Leech stood apart from them, watching and yet, without speaking, seeming to direct the whole ghastly scene.

After a few minutes, he went over to where Kostas Manou was struggling under a load of weapons, and taking some of them he set out for the cliff face followed by the others.

Douglas had wandered aimlessly round, cutting the lower identity discs from the dead men's necks. He finished up where the last jeep had crashed, and stood looking down at the dead major's body. He had never met Watkins and knew nothing about him. He wondered who he was, what was his mission, and why he now lay dead in the sand, his eyes open and surprised, a lump missing from the side of his head so that white bone and grey brain showed together, making a color scheme that looked strangely acceptable against the background of the desert floor.

He was filled with a violent fury at the massacre,

and his enforced part as a spectator but, irrationally, what raised his fury to a blind, reckless rage was the looting and the complete disregard of the dead men by Leech and his gang. And as they started to file past him on their way to the cliff, their arms filled with what they had salvaged, he raised his Sten and pulled back the cockingpiece. At the sound, they halted and turned towards him, their faces surprised and wary, and a few of them lowered what they carried to the ground.

"Bury them."

Douglas faced them across ten yards of desert, the sweat on his face growing cold as no one moved. The men's eyes switched from him to Leech and back again. They were waiting for a lead, and Leech said nothing, staring implacably at Douglas.

The sudden click of a cocked gun coming from behind him made Douglas spin round, and in the split second before he met Kafkarides' eyes staring at him over the gun the Cypriot held levelled at him, he heard a succession of clicks from the others. He turned back slowly. Boudesh, Sadok and Kostas Manou all had their guns trained on him; Hassan and Assine watched with interest; Leech smiled, tight-lipped. A second rage—at his own stupidity in not accounting for every man—swept over Douglas and, ignoring Kafkarides behind him, he spoke again, thrusting his gun forward threateningly.

"Bury them."

No one moved, and Douglas felt his bowels turn inside him. His thighs started to tremble, and he braced them, afraid that he would fall. He thrust the gun out in front of him again, and heard Leech break the silence.

"I think he means it."

Douglas stood over them for long hours in the sweltering sun, his Sten cradled in his arms, watching each grave dug, and each British soldier lowered into it. When the last corpse had been covered and the last shovel flung down in disgust, the men again picked up the gear they had salvaged and headed for the cliff. Leech waited for Douglas and fell in alongside him, speaking without looking at him.

"That wasn't very clever."

Douglas stared straight in front of him. He knew his action had been stupid. He'd held the unit up for hours, and achieved nothing constructive, but he didn't care. Leech pointed at the Sten Douglas still held in his hands.

"You'd have killed one of us—maybe two. But number three would have been you."

Douglas knew that this was as true as the stupidity of his stand, and that in fact Leech, by acquiescing and setting a lead, had saved his life. He replied without attempting to keep the bitterness from his voice.

"Thank you."

"Just try to forget all those noble sentiments—if you want to live."

"I'll manage."

They arrived at the foot of the cliff, and Douglas started to scramble up. Leech's voice came through to him from behind.

"Funny thing—survival."

CHAPTER 9

IF THE UNIT could have moved on at speed after the massacre of the British troops, it would have been easier for Douglas to view with objectivity all that had happened since leaving Masters' headquarters, but the conditions encountered after leaving the Depression made this impossible. He had little opportunity of sitting detached, the lonely commander considering what had occurred and why. From the moment they entered the Sand Sea, every man was constantly involved in the battle to force a way forward across the drifting waste.

Kafkarides and Sadok drove their vehicles with a relentless determination, fighting all the time to keep on course; at times standing behind their steering wheels forcing them in the opposite direction to the sloughing drag of the loose sand on the steep slopes of the dunes. They hardly ever covered a mile without one or other of the vehicles becoming bogged down and, the moment this occurred, the remainder of the unit started work without being told. Shovels and sand-tracks were constantly in use and, when these were of no avail and the jeep and truck were axle-deep in the sand, they had recourse to the cables and pulleys. They sweated in the sun, driving anchoring stakes deep into the sand, hauling on the cables till their muscles cracked with strain. They hammered and wrenched at the stakes to free them after their brief minutes of use. A trouble-free mile was good going: on occasions they were stuck several times within a hundred yards.

Douglas worked with the men, and as hard as they did. He recognized their expertise as they did his, but there was something about their individual approach to everything they did that was a silent denial of any form of teamwork. They worked together because it was the only way to get the job done speedily and successfully. Douglas couldn't help but admire their individuality, the way in which each man thought for himself and nearly always arrived at the right conclusion. They displayed a form of blind courage which drove them on, time after time: they didn't tackle the checks and holdups as British soldiers or workmen would—they fought them, savagely. And long after the average man would have packed in from sheer exhaustion and frustration, they threw themselves at each new task with the same energy they had shown at the beginning.

Leech helped only when it was absolutely necessary. For the remainder, he walked up and down in the sand, smoking incessantly. He seemed to regard the digging out of the vehicles, the back-breaking hauling on the cables, not as something beneath his dignity, but as something which really had nothing to do with what he was being paid for. Only when the joint efforts of the others failed to move a vehicle did he throw himself alongside them, adding the strength of his powerful arms and back to theirs.

Dust and sand filled carburetors and choked feedlines, and there were times when, waiting for Kafkarides to clear one of them, Douglas looked across the seemingly unending waste of soft sand ahead of them and wondered whether they would ever make it to the other side, to the firmer going of the Stone Desert.

There were times when he was near to despair and once, when it took them three hours to cover two hundred yards, he had a moment of regret that he had not accepted Leech's offer to pick him up on the way back. At night, he had to force himself to accept and eat the food they cooked: the temptation to throw his exhausted body down, and escape into sleep as soon as the unit halted was almost more than he could resist.

They had been in the Sand Sea for sixty hours and the going remained unchanged. Douglas looked down at his map and measured the distance they had covered. He turned to Leech.

"We've only covered eighty kilometers in the last two and a half days."

"That's quite good going."

"At this rate the war's going to be over before we get there, or they'll have used all the petrol."

"Don't worry," Leech grinned sardonically, "You'll get your medal."

They hit shale the next morning, and bowled along at a good speed. Everyone seemed more buoyant, except Leech. Douglas smiled happily as he checked his sun-compass.

"It's not going to take us long at this rate."

Leech grunted, "Wait—you've got the worst to come. Soon we'll be in the fesh-fesh."

Douglas had heard of the Stone Desert, but had never encountered it. He had thought the shale they were driving over was the beginning of it, that it might get a bit lumpier, but that would be all. Leech's words made him apprehensive, for with all his faults Douglas had yet to hear the Irishman exaggerate. If Douglas considered only that part of Leech's life which had been spent in the desert, he had to admit that Leech had material for the most terrific line-shooting, but he never discussed any of the missions he had been on, let alone boasted about them.

They hit the real fesh-fesh later in the day, and Douglas began to appreciate what Leech had meant. The vehicles bounced from ridge to ridge of solidified rock, the larger stones lying so close to each other that no driver could steer a course between them, and time and again the steering wheels were wrenched from Kafkarides' and Sadok's hands. A tire on the jeep was the first to go, and Douglas and Leech climbed down to stretch their legs while the Cypriot changed the wheel. Douglas strolled a yard or two away and sat with his back to a rock, pulling out his chess set and studying the position of the pieces. Leech watched him for a moment and then walked over to where he sat.

"Why don't you say something?"

Douglas looked up.

"What for?"

Leech's face was showing real expression for the first time. He was angry—perhaps lonely.

"I said why don't you say something? Why don't you talk like a human being?"

Douglas continued to look up at Leech: he felt that he was slowly getting on top.

"The way to survive is to watch and listen and to say nothing . . . I don't trust you, and I don't want to know you."

Leech stared down at Douglas, his face again set and impassive, and Douglas saw his hand drift towards the long knife that he'd felt at his throat only three days before.

"Is that what happened to the other British officers?"

When Leech spoke, he ignored the question.

"It's going to be a long ride."

Kafkarides threw the jack into the back of the jeep.

Douglas got to his feet, and he and Leech climbed wearily back in the vehicle.

An hour later they pulled in under the shade of a great rock for the midday halt. Boudesh went at once to the radio and commenced the tinkering which he devoted to it at every opportunity he got. Douglas and Leech sat in the shade, chewing their rations and watching Kafkarides and Sadok at work patching the tires. Sadok showed his despair with a gesture at the tires as he turned to the two captains.

"We must to find new ones."

"Why don't you use a spare?" Douglas asked.

"No more spare . . ."

Douglas looked at Leech.

"If I'd done the inspection, there'd have been enough spares."

They drove on through the burning Stone Desert for four more hours, making little ground. Although the tires burst less often than when they had been bogged down in the Sand Sea, it took longer to repair the tubes and replace the wheels. At nearly five o'clock in the afternoon they sighted a waterhole. Around it lay burned-out tanks, abandoned vehicles and the bodies of dead Italians. At that moment, a tire on the jeep went. Kafkarides drove on without stopping, the tire flapping against the rim.

Leech turned and shouted to Sadok in the truck behind.

"There are your tires—let's get them."

Douglas looked at the map and his watch. He was impatient to get on, but he knew there was no alternative: without the tires they would never make it. Kafkarides turned off the route they were following, with Sadok close behind. They stopped outside the ring of vehicles, and everyone climbed down. Douglas started to move towards the Italian vehicles and then halted, realizing that he was the only one who had moved. He glanced at the others, standing for the most part in the positions they had taken up when they had got out of the jeep and truck. His eyes swung from face to face. They were all searching the area containing the burned-out convoy, their eyes quartering the ground slowly. He felt impatience surge up inside him, but he controlled it, knowing that he had not yet seen any of them take a considered action without there being a purpose behind it.

Leech moved first, walking casually forward, his eyes darting from side to side, and the others followed him, spreading out as they entered the ring of vehicles. Kafkarides, Sadok, and Boudesh examined the wheels of the trucks; Hassan and Assine stood apart from the others in the center of the circle, holding hands, their eyes flashing from dead body to dead body. Assine gave a sudden cry and darted forward, pouncing on the arm of an Italian corpse, hanging down from the side of a truck; he scrabbled at the strap holding a watch to the dead man's wrist. He got it off, held it to his ear, wound it, listened again, shook it, and threw it away in disgust. He turned to where he had left Hassan, but his friend was no longer there: he was already busy unstrapping a watch for himself, undisturbed by the stench from the body he crouched over.

Douglas cast a cursory glance at the first two vehicles he passed. On one, the tires were all flat: on the other, they were too large for either the jeep or the truck. He spotted another he thought would do and approached it. He was joined by Leech as he stood a yard or so back from it, gauging its size. Leech spoke with certainty.

"They'll do for the truck."

Douglas turned away to collect a jack from their

own vehicles and spotted one in the sand only a few paces from where he stood. He moved quickly, bending to pick it up, but even as his fingers closed round it his hand was trapped by Leech's suede boot bearing down on it, and he heard Leech's level voice from above him.

"Keep perfectly still—don't move."

Leech raised his voice to a higher key, "Kostas Manou!"

Douglas had reacted instantly to the warning note in Leech's voice, freezing where he crouched, and only as he sensed Kostas Manou's cautious approach did he look up, very slowly raising his head. He met Leech's eyes staring down at him, and glimpsed the Greek's circling approach; farther away he could see Boudesh, Sadok, and Kafkarides, all looking towards where he crouched, their eyes glued to his hand, Leech's foot, and the jack. As they watched, they backed very slowly to the cover of the armored vehicles to one side of them. Douglas felt the saliva dry in his mouth, and his throttle constricted as if gripped by a powerful hand; then Kostas Manou was kneeling at his side, sweat on his face, rubbing his hands slowly together to dry them.

The Greek lowered his hands to one end of the jack, stroking the sand away very gently. He moved his fingers a few inches and repeated the same delicate movement, fondling the desert floor like a lover stirring a woman's desire. Again he moved, and again. Douglas looked at his face, seeing the strain behind the mask of sand, damp with sweat. He looked up. Leech's face bore the one expression to which Douglas had become used: blank except for the sardonic twist of the lips. He looked harder and saw that Leech's eyes were changed, the expression in them hard to define. It somehow combined amusement and resignation, as if

Leech saw humor in a situation in which he had deliberately placed himself.

Douglas dropped his glance to where Kostas Manou was still at work. He saw the Greek's hands freeze suddenly into perfect stillness, and flashed a quick look at his face. Kostas Manou's eyes were closed, and his lips moved silently. Douglas knew instinctively that he was praying, and was astonished that he felt no surprise. When Kostas Manou opened his eyes he looked first at Douglas, and in them was the second comradely look of sharing that Douglas had seen since the expedition had set out. The first he had seen had been in the same eyes, when he and Kostas had worked together to get the vehicles up the cliff from the Qattara Depression. Kostas Manou had been the only man who believed in the possibility of getting the trucks to the top of the cliff.

Kostas Manou looked up at Leech and nodded once. He looked down again at the sand in front of him, and his fingers moved even slower than before. They checked once, then dug deeper into the sand, drawing it away so that the sand above his fingers dropped into the cavity he had made, gravity seeming to claim each grain. Douglas saw the first inch of the thin wire appear, and his heart jumped once at the confirmation of what they had suspected. Kostas Manou took his hands away and rubbed them together for the second time, his eyes still fixed on the wire. He set to, working methodically, easing the sand away at a depth of a couple of inches so that the sand above dropped into the empty space below, and the length of wire grew slowly.

There was nothing Douglas could do, and as an engineer he recognized it; he tried to divorce his mind from the operation in hand, and he looked away: if he was to be blown to eternity, there was nothing to be gained by looking at the source of his destruction. His eyes travelled from Leech's boot to the corduroyed leg above it, and he found himself thinking of the look he had seen in Leech's eyes when he had first looked up. If Kostas Manou managed successfully to de-fuse the booby-trap, Leech would have succeeded in saving Douglas' life, and Douglas wondered why. His death would give Leech much greater freedom of action: there would no longer be any question about who commanded the expedition. If he had read them right, Leech's eyes had told a tale of disbelief in himself, an amused contempt for his own action, and a careless resignation to the consequences to himself of what he had done. Douglas found himself considering the possibility that Leech never got very far beyond considering the precise moment in time that concerned him.

He heard a sudden intake of breath from Kostas Manou, and looked down. Two to three feet of wire lay exposed, and the end farthest from the jack disappeared under a tin lid. Kostas Manou rubbed his hands together for the third time and looked from under his brows, first at Douglas, then up at Leech. He looked down and grasped each end of the tin lid, firmly, without moving it forward, back, or sideways. He was going to lift it straight upwards, and Douglas found himself dwelling on the possibility that there might be a double booby-trap, the second one attached to the tin lid. If there was, it would be all over in a second, and three dead or terribly maimed men would be lying where they now crouched or stood. The specialist in him made him watch Kostas Manou with more curiosity than fear.

The Greek's fingers, hooked under the lid, showed suddenly white, then he was lifting it vertically, exposing the detonating device; the end of the wire attached to the un-split safety-pin. He put the lid down carefully to one side of him, and reaching to his belt he pulled from it a pair of pliers. He gripped the pin, where it joined the wire, with the fingers of his left hand; with his right he closed the pliers round the pin on the far side of the detonating device. It was a "puller-type," needing only movement from the far end to pull the loose pin free of the striker it held up. Once the pin was clear, the spring attachment would pull the firing-pin on to the detonator below, and the whole explosive charge would go up.

Douglas watched the pliers as they closed round the pin.

All three were unprepared for the blasting, explosive roar from behind them. Douglas had expected a blinding flash and oblivion if Kostas Manou had failed. His eyes closed, the lids jammed till they hurt, and his facial muscles stretched back, pulling his lips away from his teeth, his shoulders hunched, and he sunk his head between them like a tortoise.

"Still. . . . STILL!"

Leech's words broke through to him as he waited for the blast, and for the tearing round-balled shrapnel to rip into his body. For a lingering second of time he was unable to open his eyes, his preconceived certainty of what was to follow over-riding and swamping the contradiction carried in Leech's warning. He opened his eyes and found them still fixed on the safety-pin, the hole in the striker, and Kostas Manou's fingers wrapped round the pliers. He watched the jaws of the pliers close tighter, and followed the powerful movement of the Greek's wrist as he bent the safety-pin till it was impossible for it to be pulled through the hole in the striker. Leech lifted his foot, Kostas Manou stood up, wiping the sweat from his face, and Douglas followed suit. They all turned in the direction from which the explosion had come. Hassan lay stretched on his back on the ground, one arm flung out, the fingers still clutching a wrist watch, his white burnous, from pelvis to breastbone stained bright red with his blood. His head was thrown back and his eyes closed. Assine was still a couple of yards from him, but running to where Hassan lay. He threw himself to the ground beside his friend, grasping his hand and calling his name. When he got no reply, he rocked back on his heels, lifted his head and howled like an animal. He leaned forward suddenly and lifted Hassan in his arms, keening over him, his sense of loss striking a chill into Douglas as he strode towards them. He arrived a second after Sadok, and held back while the Tunisian pulled Assine away from his friend and bent over Hassan. He looked up. "He is living."

They cut away the burnous and looked down at the swamp of blood oozing from Hassan's belly, ripped and torn by the blast. Douglas shouted for dressings, and as they were produced and applied he recognized their inadequacy.

"Is that all you've got?"

Only Leech answered, his voice betraying nothing beyond the actual meaning of his words.

"We had more. They were in the wireless truck."

Douglas looked back to Hassan, now conscious, his eyes mirroring the terrible pain he felt. He helped Sadok get Hassan to the truck while the others salvaged serviceable tires from the Italian vehicles, Assine hovering round them as they moved his friend and lover, his keening a high-pitched accompaniment to the sustained groans of Hassan.

Leech joined Douglas as the remainder of the unit

brought in the last of the tires. He picked up the map lying on Douglas' seat and looked at it.

"We're getting near. We'd better start traveling by night."

Douglas nodded his agreement. "We'll eat now and travel as soon as we finish."

CHAPTER 10

By THE TIME they started the night drive, Hassan was a little quieter, the first, excruciating pain of his wounds eased by rest and care but, within minutes of the vehicles moving off, Douglas heard his cries as the truck bounced over the rocky desert. He tried to shut his ears to them but, even when they died out, the continuous keening of Assine came through to him. He forced his mind to concentrate on the task ahead and the route to be maintained despite the frequent deviations made necessary by outcrops of rock, some of them eight and ten feet high. And he fought his own exhaustion, made worse by the shock of the afternoon's experience.

It was after midnight when Leech tapped Kafkarides on the shoulder and called to him to stop. Douglas looked round at Leech and saw him looking over his shoulder at the truck behind. It had stopped, and Kafkarides reversed slowly towards it. As they drew close to it, Sadok's voice came to them out of the night.

"If we go on, Hassan will die."

Douglas looked at Leech.

"Can't we leave them?"

When he answered, Leech's voice had a faint, jeering note in it.

"It's a question of getting back; I could do it—but you couldn't."

Recognizing the truth, both of what Leech said, and

the implication in his voice, Douglas turned to his map and tapped it.

"We're only twenty miles from the German supply road."

Leech was silent for a few moments, thinking about it, seeing possibilities, and wondering exactly what Douglas had in mind.

"So?"

"I don't know yet, but a supply road means vehicles, medical supplies, perhaps a doctor. There must be something."

"All right, let's see what we can do."

Leech leaned forward and waved Kafkarides on. They moved off, bouncing over the rocks, their direction changed, taking a more direct route to the north.

They stopped just before first light, and Douglas and Leech studied the map. Douglas asked:

"Where do you think we are?"

"About there." Leech thrust his forefinger at a point three miles south of the supply road.

"Then this is as good a place to leave them as any. At least he'll have some shade."

They left the truck and the three Arabs, and the five of them headed on in the jeep to the north.

At the foot of a long ridge, running away out of sight in both directions, Leech called on Kafkarides to stop, and he leaned forward to the map in Douglas' hands.

"This is the ridge. The road's the other side of it."

He sat back again, his face amused, waiting for Douglas to take over. Douglas accepted the challenge. It had been his idea to move up to the German supply route, and it would have to be his operation from now on. He had only the roughest plan ready in his mind, but he stepped out of the jeep with what he hoped was confidence and beckoned to the others. They all followed him without question, a different look on every face.

The ridge was low, but high enough to cover the jeep and their movements, and it took them only a minute or two to scramble to the top and conceal themselves behind the cactus scrub, planted by the Italians in their pioneering days to prevent erosion. Douglas listened to the sound of traffic beyond the ridge, his head cocked to one side, his eyes on Leech lolling comfortably on one elbow a yard below him. On Leech's face was a look both amused and speculative: apart from his cynicism, he was interested in how Douglas would tackle the problem, and he had no intention of interfering unless he saw the whole unit endangered for a hare-brained scheme. He intended playing it off the cuff.

Douglas waited until the sound of the vehicles on the road beyond the ridge had sunk and died to the east. He eased himself forward between two cacti, and raising his glasses he looked up the road to the west, to the way from which Rommel's supplies and services must come. If something moved back from the east, from the direction of the front, at the wrong moment, then he was in trouble. He turned to the two men nearest him. They were Boudesh and Kafkarides.

"You," he pointed to Boudesh, "rip your trousers, turn them up and get a bandage round your leg." He swung his eyes to Kafkarides, expecting opposition, but mentally holding Kostas Manou in reserve. "You come with us."

Kafkarides grinned a little wider than usual, and looking back up the road Douglas wondered what the exaggerated grin meant. He spotted a convoy of half-tracks filled with troops coming towards them, and he sank back out of sight, watching Boudesh bandaging his leg. He tried not to look at Leech.

It took five or six minutes for the convoy to pass and, when the last vehicle had gone by, Douglas looked again this time in both directions. The road was clear. He signalled to the other two to follow him. Easing himself between the cacti he slid down the slope to the rainditch at the bottom of the ridge, Boudesh and Kafkarides tumbling in beside him.

He looked cautiously out, spotted empty trucks returning from the front and ducked back into the ditch. When they were past, he looked again and saw three vehicles coming from the west. He used his glasses and identified them as armored cars. He cursed softly as he slid back into cover.

After the armor had gone by, there was no movement on the road for a long time. Douglas looked several times at the Lebanese and the Cypriot. He had intended telling them nothing till the last moment, hoping to give them no chance to think about it, but each time he caught their eyes he became more conscious that he was not dealing with private soldiers or junior NCOs. The calculated impassivity of Boudesh influenced him more than the constant challenge of the Cypriot's staring eyes and the grin which no longer affected him, since it was as permanent as the nose on Kafkarides' face.

"I want an ambulance, if I can get one," he said, "but we might have to settle for something less. I'll stop them—Boudesh is the decoy. You," he nodded at Kafkarides, "support him—hold him up, but be ready for anything."

He waited for their response, but there was none. They had heard him, they looked at him, but their expressions never changed. He turned back to the road. For all he knew, when the moment came, he might be stepping out in front of an enemy vehicle alone, unsupported.

A German staff-car came by very fast, and then Douglas picked out through his glasses what he had been waiting for, the Red Cross markings on a lone ambulance coming from the west: one from the east would have most likely been filled with casualties from the front.

Douglas moved out from the ditch: he beckoned to the other two before stepping into the center of the road and holding up his hand. From the corner of his eyes he saw them follow him, and he was filled with a sense of relief that for a moment weakened him. He glanced quickly at Boudesh and Kafkarides standing behind him, the left arm of the Lebanese resting round the Cypriot's shoulders, and he moved farther out into the road so that those in the ambulance could see the casualty clearly.

The ambulance came on very fast, and for a frightening few seconds Douglas wondered whether it was going to stop; then he heard the brakes going on and the ambulance was slowing. It didn't stop before it got to them, but came to a halt the full length of its body past them. Douglas turned and waited, his body tense.

The escort wrenched open the right hand door and dropped on to the road, moving quickly towards where Douglas waited. The driver a pace or two behind him. Douglas moved slightly to one side, a smile of greeting on his face. He had cleared Kafkarides' field of fire, and he nodded once to the Cypriot. The hand concealed behind Boudesh swung up between the two men and Kafkarides gunned the escort down from a distance of three yards. The driver stopped flatfooted behind the falling body of his escort, his eyes wide and his mouth open. He turned and started to run, his limbs uncoordinated and flapping. Douglas put a burst into his back before he'd taken two steps.

Leech and Kostas Manou were on the road before Douglas had lowered his gun. Leech threw him one look of approval.

"You're learning."

They dragged the bodies of the dead Germans off the road and heaved them into the ditch. Kostas Manou and Boudesh headed up the ridge to where they'd left the jeep, and Douglas and Leech climbed into the front of the ambulance. They set off down the road to where a cut in the bank opened the way to the other side of the ridge. As the ambulance started up, Kafkarides jumped on to the running-board. Leech yelled at him:

"Get in the back."

They slowed down while he climbed in, then they were off at a breakneck pace, up through the cut, a slight deviation to the west to obscure any view of them from the road, and out into the desert after the jeep, already heading back to the truck and the three Arabs.

Sadok spotted them coming from a long way off, and he eased himself out of the driver's seat till he was behind the machine gun mounting, lowering the gun and levelling it at the oncoming vehicles. When he recognized the jeep, he lowered the butt of the Vickers MMG, his thumbs falling like lazy leaves from the thumb-piece which, depressed, could pump six hundred rounds of .303 a minute through the water-cooled barrel.

The jeep and the ambulance swung in alongside the stationary truck with dash: both drivers conscious of success and displaying their satisfaction in the way they handled their vehicles.

As Leech cut the engine of the ambulance, he and

Douglas became aware of the commotion in the back of it, and they looked at each other, their eyes locking in speculation. They both reached for the handles of the doors, throwing them open and jumping down into the sand. Douglas rushed to the back of the ambulance, perhaps not more concerned, but certainly less conscious of danger than Leech who moved first out into the desert, away from the vehicle, so that he approached from the side at a wider angle and with a better field of view.

Douglas swung open the rear doors of the ambulance, stepping to one side and drawing his pistol.

The unlocking of the doors was like lifting the lid on a human volcano—two figures erupted from the back of the ambulance and landed in the sand, fighting even while they were still in the air. They struggled to their feet, and the watchers recognized the second figure as a woman, a German nurse of Amazon proportions. As they watched, she caught Kafkarides with a vicious right swing that started from behind her own right hip. He dropped in the sand, but almost at once was on his feet, his eyes still staring and his grin still fixed. He groped towards her, his hands extended, his fingers hooked. The nurse sank back, her weight taken on her left leg, balancing herself, and as Kafkarides came within range she kicked him viciously in the testicles with her right foot. He screamed and clutched himself, staggering on legs which somehow still kept him on his feet. The nurse changed the position of her feet and swung again, catching Kafkarides flush on the point. Still gripping his balls, he dropped into the sand—out cold.

Douglas stepped forward, his movements disoriented by the unexpectedness of what he had witnessed. He laid his hand on the nurse's shoulder. She turned and hit him flush on the chin. He staggered back, recovered himself and closed with her. A second later he was flying through the air, but this time the nurse followed up her attack and fell on him, her fists flailing and her square-toed shoes driving at his body.

Leech, once he had assessed the situation, had come to rest, leaning against the back of the ambulance, and now, his face showing amusement, he moved forward. With his left hand he gripped the nurse by the shoulder. He swung her round towards him, and in the same easy movement he hit her once on the chin with his clenched right fist, and watched her fall unconscious over the sprawling Douglas. Leech grinned.

"Don't you know how to handle a woman?"

He took a sub-machine gun from one of the men and swung it on the nurse as she came round and forced herself into a sitting position. Her eyes opened wide with apprehension and fear, but she didn't cry out. She sat staring up at Leech, hate slowly replacing the fear in her eyes as he pulled back the cocking-piece of the gun. Douglas moved forward, calling out to Leech.

"No!" And then in a lower voice, emotion gone from it, using reason to convince: "She can take care of Hassan." He gestured to where Sadok and Boudesh carried the Senussi on a stretcher to the back of the ambulance, Assine walking alongside it, clasping Hassan's hand in his own.

Leech swung the barrel of his gun towards the stretcher as he spoke to the nurse.

"When he dies, you die. Understand?"

He brought the gun back till it was aimed at her, thrusting it forward threateningly.

The nurse nodded her head slowly.

They drove quickly back into the desert till they were again on their original route, and in the afternoon they bivouacked, camouflaging the vehicles. They fed and, with the exception of Boudesh and the German nurse, lay down to sleep, preparing themselves for the long night drive. Douglas lay in the shade, his body tired, his mind active, churning over the events of the past few days. They had travelled hundreds of miles across dried salt quagmire, the Sand Sea and the fesh-fesh. They had butchered six Arabs in cold blood, because of a careless mistake which no other member of the unit but he would have made. They had lain in a position of safety and watched the massacre of nearly half a hundred British officers and men, and his attempt to warn them had been thwarted by a calculated act of Leech's. He realized that had he been permitted to fire the warning shots the outcome would have been much the same. A single vehicle and the men in it *might* have escaped, a few Germans *might* have been killed. Had he acted as instinct prompted him, only one thing was certain, and in retrospect he recognized this. The operation for which he was responsible would have ceased to have even the slenderest chance of success. He tried to look at the military situation as a whole, to evaluate the consequences of what had occurred, and to weigh them against the main objective: the defeat of Rommel and his Afrika Korps. With Africa freed of Axis troops, an entire British army and all the shipping required to maintain it would be freed for the attack on Hitler's Europe. The British naval command of the Mediterranean was now firmly established, re-supply of the Axis armies was difficult and at times impossible. The destruction of the huge petrol-dump which was the objective of the unit he commanded could well be the final straw which broke Rommel's back. The lives of a hundred men, a thousand men, were relatively unimportant, for their deaths might save the lives of tens of thousands of men of all nationalities. This was the rational way of thinking about it. Douglas tried but he couldn't accept the means. Intellectually he could admit the logic apparent in Leech's actions, provided he accepted that the actions themselves were directed towards the main objective and nothing else. This, he couldn't do. He and Leech had had similar backgrounds and upbringing, they had been to the same sort of school—perhaps Leech's had been better—but somewhere along the line Leech's thinking had changed. Douglas was still controlled by standards of conduct which Leech had learned but no longer recognized, or perhaps believed to have no validity. Christ! There must be some principles, some codes of conduct, even in war.

Douglas threw aside the blanket which covered him and stood up. He walked over to where Boudesh tinkered at the radio. He stopped behind the Lebanese and watched as Boudesh measured across two points with his gauge. He saw him press the morse-code lever down and get a positive response on the meter. He saw Boudesh's smile.

"Any luck?" he asked.

"The receiver's finished, but I think we can transmit."

"Let's try tonight. What time are we due to transmit?"

Boudesh took the card from his pocket with the times and wavelengths written on it. He passed it to Douglas without looking at him. Douglas glanced down at it, reading aloud.

'Two-seven-eight cycles at twenty-thirty hours." He looked at Boudesh, "we'll try before we move off."

The Lebanese grunted, and Douglas moved away from him, back to his blanket and the rest he knew he needed.

At eight-fifteen, Boudesh wakened because he knew he must. He stood up, rubbing the sleep from his eyes with one hand and clutching at his crutch with the other. He eased his pants from where his sweat stuck them round his groin, and he pulled down at the clinging drill trousers. He looked at the wristwatch he had cut from the arm of a Panzer captain, still dying when he took it for his own. He looked round, his big head swinging slowly, taking in the sleeping camp: he picked out movement under the canvas awning covering Hassan. He watched the German nurse as she bent over the Senussi guide. He could see her deft movements as she changed the dressings on the Arab's belly and chest, and he recognized the promise of muscular contraction in the swing of her buttocks and the line of her thighs pressing against her short skirt. The hand that had eased his pants stroked the thrusting pressure of his rising sex. His eyes hooded and his breathing grew faster, the intake and out-thrust of his breath keeping time with the throbbing blood which had changed his sex into a weapon ready to be plunged into the body he watched.

He breathed out in a long sibilant hiss that broke the syncopation of his breath and blood, and he moved forward.

The German nurse gathered together the bloodied dressings in a surgical tray and moved away from the environs of the camp to bury them. She glanced only to her right and left, a brief recognition that she stood in some danger; then she walked on, the tray held in both hands in front of her.

Boudesh walked after her, wireless forgotten, sex and the satisfaction of his bursting lust dominant in his mind. From the corner of his eye he spotted Kafka-rides break through a gap in the vehicles in a crouching run, but he maintained his pace. He was bigger than Kafkarides, stronger: if they arrived together, it would be he who took her first.

She bent down, clearing a space in the sand to bury the dressings and Boudesh stopped for a moment, watching the length of her bare legs increase as the hem of her skirt raised. They were strong legs, muscular: not feminine, but holding out the promise of participation. If she fought him, they would become part of the sexual act, something better than the limp parting of limbs which was all that the Arab whores had to offer.

He watched Kafkarides' rush, the hand that clamped over her mouth and the other that clutched ineffectively at her breasts as she swung free and chopped him in the gut with her left hand. And then Kostas Manou was in the picture, coming past Boudesh like a sprinter in the last few yards of a race. The Greek launched himself like a rugby player making a tackle: grasping her high round the thighs, but allowing his clasped hands to slide down her legs till they closed, trapping her ankles and throwing her to the ground.

She landed on her back, her arms flailing at Kafkarides, her legs striking out at Kostas Manou. Boudesh closed up to within a yard of the struggling trio, his hips thrust forward, inches in front of his barrel chest. He looked down at them struggling in the sand, at Kafkarides' grin as he looked up at Boudesh, his weight on the nurse's left arm, his two hands clasped below her left knee, forcing her leg outwards. He read Kafkarides as easily as he would the headlines in a tabloid newspaper. The promise in the staring eyes was either so true as not to be believed, or a complete lie. He reached for the buckle on his belt. Kafkarides would either have an orgasm while he watched Boudesh rape the German nurse, or, given the opportunity, he would copulate with her himself till he fell away from her without coming. It depended entirely upon what drug he had taken last, and how long ago. Boudesh undid the buttons of his flies and looked at Kostas Manou. The Greek met his eyes and smiled, holding the nurse's right leg out and nodding his head at the white-knickered crutch as he might have done had what lay beyond the white cotton, been a bottle of Retsina. He was the host, and he was inviting Boudesh to be his guest. Boudesh let go of his trousers, allowing them to fall to his braced knees. He waited for one of them to rip aside the cotton knickers.

Hassan, his eyes dull with pain and a new affection that was unrelated to sex, had watched the nurse as she walked into the desert. He saw the slow approach of Boudesh, the circling movement of Kafkarides, the flying rush of Kostas Manou, and he reached for his pistol. He glanced down at Assine, asleep in the sand below where he lay on the raised stretcher, and at Assine's right hand still clutching the metal runner supporting the canvas beneath him. He raised his head, the pistol in his right hand, his left grasping it at the wrist, steadying his aim. He sighted the pistol carefully, the effort of holding his head up bringing the blood from his lungs into his mouth. He squeezed the trigger and fell back.

The bullet hit Boudesh in the right buttock as he prepared to lower himself between the forcibly parted legs of the German nurse.

The shot brought Douglas and Leech out of their blankets, Douglas in a stumbling run, his mouth agape, his mind tumbling in an effort to assess the situation before he was fully awake; Leech in a single swift movement that carried him yards from where he had been lying, a pistol in his hand before he was free of the blanket that covered him. They walked cautiously forward till they stood together looking out into the desert, and at the scene in front of them. Boudesh, his trousers round his ankles, and the German nurse applying a dressing to his buttock. Kafkarides, resting on his elbows in the sand, his knees raised and parted, and Kostas Manou two yards away from the other three, his head back, laughing like a drunk in the front row at a music-hall.

Douglas spoke because he had waited too long for Leech, his question compulsive, blurted out and half checked as he sought to make it carry a greater meaning than the words expressed.

"What happened?"

Boudesh turned his head and looked down towards the nurse at work on the flesh wound in the right check of his backside. She met his eyes in a flash of agreement and turned back to his buttock.

He looked at Douglas.

"Nothing."

CHAPTER 11

DOUGLAS WALKED OVER to the wireless set, wondering what was the first cause which had resulted in the extraordinary tableau he had just witnessed. He reached out to the transmitter, his mind cavorting at the possibilities. He glanced at the card, tuned to the correct cycle, and started to tap out his message in morse.

Leech came up to where Douglas stood, and asked, "What are you telling them?"

"I'm explaining why we're six days late."

Leech snorted gently at Douglas' need to explain.

"Keep it short," he said, "we don't want to be monitored by the Germans."

They drove on through the night, the going getting better as they progressed. Douglas looked constantly at his map, checking their position: Leech, behind him, in the back of the jeep, unconcerned with what the map might tell him, peered round with an anxious, animal alertness.

Half-an-hour after first light, Douglas signalled Kafkarides to stop, and as the Cypriot braked to a standstill Douglas turned to Leech, nodding his head at the long ridge in front of them. Leech nodded back, a reluctant admission that Douglas' pathfinding was accurate.

They climbed down and stretched themselves. Douglas looked back to where the ambulance and supply truck had halted. Boudesh was at the wheel of the ambulance, Kostas Manou by his side. Sadok and Assine were in the stores truck, bringing up the rear. He let his eyes dwell on each of them in turn. Christ! They were tough bastards. In a fight to the finish, he felt he would sooner have them on his side than any other equivalent number of men—provided they had no other way out.

Douglas caught up with Leech who was already striding towards the ridge. They went on together, crawling the last few yards, easing themselves into a position of observation without showing more than their eyes and the tops of their heads. It was there, half a mile in front of them, the details instantly recognizable from the photographs taken by the Majabra tribesmen.

Its center feature was the tall, thin frame of the windpump, its blades turned south to the hot wind blowing up from the heart of the desert, its vane pointing like a signpost to the Mediterranean; around it, the great petrol storage-tanks and thousands of forty-gallon drums, stacked tier upon tier like the stepped side of a pyramid; around the perimeter of the complex the long barrels of 88 mm anti-aircraft guns pointed at the sky; and the glint of barbed-wire showed in a great arc between the watching men and the dump. Reaching for his fieldglasses, Douglas spoke to Leech.

"That's it."

He adjusted the glasses slowly so that he could take in the small detail, picking out, one by one, the German sentries. He made a quick sketch of the dump on a message-pad before sliding below the crest of the ridge. He and Leech walked back to where the unit waited, standing idly round the vehicles, with the exception of Assine who had joined the German nurse and Hassan in the back of the ambulance.

Douglas called them all together and issued his orders for the operation. It would have to be conducted under cover of darkness, for he reckoned that the German unit guarding the dump would be at least of company strength, plus the crews of the anti-aircraft guns. Even with the element of surprise in their favor, they would stand no chance of breaking into the dump by force of arms and carrying out the demolition. At night, with only the sentries to contend with, he considered they had at least an even chance of success; a narrow route cut through the wire, a sentry or two eliminated and the charges placed.

By the middle of the afternoon, nearly all their arrangements were completed, and Douglas strolled round the small camp, stopping for a word with the men—with Sadok, measuring the length of fuses for the explosives laid out round him, and Kostas Manou packing his equipment into a haversack. He watched Boudesh and Kafkarides, their explosives loaded, ease their packs on to their backs and stand shrugging them down, gauging the weight. He looked into the back of the ambulance where the nurse sat with Hassan, and then he wandered away to where Leech sat frowning up at the sky.

As he approached Leech, and before he had asked the question he intended, Assine came running towards them, calling out as he ran.

"Big wind coming."

Leech was on his feet, shouting to the men to dig in and prepare for the storm before the implication of Assine's words had registered with Douglas. For thirty seconds he watched flat-footed as the men threw themselves at the vehicles, stretching canvas and sacking over the stores, and lashing down. He turned and looked into the desert, seeing the sand begin to whip into the air, forming shapes which jerked like paper kites in a high wind. He could hear the sound of the rushing air as it raced towards them, and as the sand it carried rose higher the sky darkened.

The storm hit them even as Douglas watched it coming, and he rushed to help as the coverings were secured and the vehicles backed end to end. When they had done all they could, the men climbed into the back of the ambulance and Douglas and Leech into the front.

The two of them sat in silence for over an hour, watching the storm as it built up to a whirling intensity, maintaining its howling peak without a let-up. By straining their eyes they could see for about ten yards, and that was all, beyond this the wind-driven sand had the appearance of solidity, a wall whose surface leaped and changed shape without ever receding, and the wall continued over their heads like the close dome of a cathedral. The possibilities offered by the storm occurred to Douglas as he watched the obscuring circle of dancing sand, and he wondered whether Leech was considering the same thing. He turned to where Leech sat at his side, his dark eyes staring through the windscreen of the ambulance, his sand-encrusted face expressionless.

"Are you thinking what I'm thinking?"

Leech met his glance, surprise showing in his eyes, his mouth quirked.

"We go in now?"

"Why not?" Douglas asked, "It's perfect cover."

"You won't be very popular."

"With them or with you?"

Leech grinned. "Dont worry about me—you worry about them."

They got out into the storm and groped their way to

the back doors of the vehicle. Douglas opened them and climbed in, followed by Leech. They stood for a moment, stooped in the bad light, looking round at the men huddled together against the sides of the ambulance, and at the German nurse changing Hassan's dressings, Douglas put into his voice every scrap of authority he could summon up, conscious of the dangerous implication in Leech's warning to him of how his change of plan would be received by the remainder of the unit.

"We're going in under cover of this storm. Cut your fuses to fifteen minutes and be ready to go in five."

All heads but one swung towards him, but that was the only movement. He stood quite still, his face set, studying theirs. Kafkarides grinned a little wider; Boudesh moved only his head, waiting as if he expected Douglas to continue talking, or somebody else to say something; Sadok looked past him at Leech, his brows raised, his eyes enquiring; then Kostas Manou started to move, drawing one leg under him as if about to get up, but he stopped, his shoulders thrown forward, the upward thrust of his bent leg checked, and his eyes followed the direction of Sadok's—over Douglas' shoulder to where Leech stood just inside the doors he had closed. Assine didn't move at all, but stayed where he was, his eyes on Hassan's; Hassan's hand in his.

Douglas spoke again: "Right. Let's get moving." Kostas Manou was nearly committed, he counted Kafkarides and Boudesh as Leech's men, and this left him only Sadok as a counter-weight. He addressed himself directly to the Tunisian.

"Sadok—tie and gag the nurse."

He couldn't see Leech, or the nod of acquiescence the Irishman directed at the others, but he saw with relief the sudden movements as they started to get to their feet, and he recognized their reluctance. The dangers of the operation mattered less to them than the discomfort of fighting their way through the storm to carry it out.

He stepped to one side as Kostas Manou, Kafkarides, and Boudesh filed past him: he waited while Assine kissed Hassan's cheek and muttered his farewell; and he watched the nurse fasten the last safety-pin to the covering bandage. And then Sadok had her by the arm, pulling her towards the upright of the top bunk. She started to resist, but Sadok thrust his face into hers, parting his lips in a silent snarl that had a more convincing effect than any physical aggression would have done. Satisfied that the Tunisian would have no trouble, Douglas followed the others into the storm.

He watched the rest of the unit groping in the backs of the jeep and truck for their weapons, the packs of explosive, and their reserve ammunition. He saw them lay out the stores, Leech check them, and each start to help another into his equipment. An afterthought occurring to him, he climbed back into the ambulance. The German nurse's wrists were secured to the head-piece of the top bunk, and Sadok was forcing a gag into her mouth. He waited until the Tunisian had finished before speaking.

"Tell Hassan to kill her if she causes trouble."

Sadok nodded, and bending over the Senussi he spoke quickly, the guttural click of the Arabic consonants sounding like silenced pistol shots, and he slid a long knife into Hassan's right hand.

Douglas and Sadok rejoined the others, and while Sadok got together his kit, Douglas divided the party into two. He detailed Kostas Manou to accompany himself and Sadok in the lead, Boudesh, Kafkarides, and Assine to follow a few paces behind, under Leech.

The Tunisian came back, loaded with explosives. Douglas raised a hand to Leech, and they all stumbled forward into the driving sand, their eyes and noses covered against the gritty blast.

CHAPTER 12

THEY TRUDGED THROUGH the stinging sand, heads
pulled down between hunched shoulders and half-
turned to the right, away from the direction of the
driving storm. It was darker than night, and the
wind-driven sand, biting into their left cheeks made
them unconsciously move away from it to the north, so
that Douglas had constantly to refer to the luminous
hands of his compass to keep them on course. It took
them half-an-hour to cover the first five or six hundred
yards. Kostas Manou was in the lead, ready to cut a
passage through the wire when they came to it. Douglas followed two paces behind, and he saw the Greek
stop suddenly in his tracks, one arm flying out in a
warning gesture to those behind him. Douglas halted
at once and signalled to the remainder to do the same.
Turning back, he watched Kostas Manou swinging his
head slowly from side to side, searching the ground:
then Kostas Manou was beckoning to him gently to
come up to where he stood. Douglas closed the gap
between them.

Kostas Manou pointed down at the desert floor, six
inches to the right of his foot, and Douglas followed
the direction of his hand. He saw at once the horned
circumference of the mine cleared of sand by the
driving wind so that even the dark metal plate below
the horns lay naked to his eye. Kostas Manou pointed
again, farther ahead and to the left, and then beyond it
and back to the right. The force of the wind had laid
bare the minefield, slicing off the concealing cover

smoothed over the mines by the German engineers.

Douglas nodded at the Greek and signalled him forward. Kostas Manou moved off cautiously, bent almost double, his eyes searching the ground. Douglas turned carefully and looked over his shoulder, finding that Leech had moved up in front of Sadok. He pointed at the mine and then moved off after Kostas Manou, keeping him in sight. Leech showed the mine to Sadok and followed Douglas, and the mimed warning was relayed back to the others.

They made their way very slowly through the minefield, but it was narrow and at last they were clear of it and approaching the wire. They stopped just short of the first apron and lay down while Kostas Manou shrugged off his pack and took his wire-cutters from his belt. He set to work expertly but very carefully, finding that not only was the wire booby-trapped, but that the area of desert over which it was laid had been planted with anti-personnel mines. Douglas followed him through the gap in the wire, stopping often while Kostas Manou turned back the barbed strands, hooking the ends away from the path he'd cleared, or altered his route to avoid a mine. Twice, when no alternative was open to him, he had to lift mines and place them to one side of the gap, but at last they were all through the wire and gathered together on the far side at the foot of the low hill with the petrol dump above them.

Douglas peered up at it, realizing that either the storm was abating a little, making it lighter, or the fact that their objective was raised above them, in some degree silhouetted, made it easier for him to pick out lines of approach. He had started to turn to Leech, when he spotted the first petrol drum come bounding down the hill to their right. It came in great leaps, driven by the storm and thrown into the air by the broken ground: it cleared the wire a few yards away from where the unit crouched, and seconds after it disappeared from their view they heard an explosion as it bounded into the minefield. It was followed by others, some checked by the wire, some like the first clearing the wire and hitting one of the mines beyond it. Douglas crouched low, his eyes straining into the spiralling sand, trying to spot any movement made by the Germans who must have been aroused by the explosions. He could see nothing, but made up his mind to wait although he could feel Leech moving impatiently at his side. He decided there must have been a pile of empty drums waiting to be filled, and that it was these that had been driven by the force of the storm into the minefield. If the Germans realized what had happened, then all would be well, but he intended giving them an opportunity to settle down again before moving up to the attack. He filled in time by giving each of the unit specific instruction as to their objectives.

Surprised, but pleased that the explosions had sparked off no reaction from the Germans, Douglas decided that enough time had been wasted, and he gave his final instruction to the waiting men crouched round him.

"Plant your charges. Back here in fifteen minutes."

He watched them set out up the hill, some crawling, some half crouched, and he followed their general direction, but taking the line he had reserved for himself, one which led him to a huge steel petrol-storage tank, its bulk showing through the storm-borne sand like a giant gasometer.

He reached the top of the hill without trouble and moved into the shelter of a German truck standing under stretched camouflaged netting. He slid under the netting to one side of it and eased the pack of explosive off his back. He had started to undo the straps when his eyes picked out, under the chassis of the truck, the straddled legs of a man standing on the far side of it. He took in the German boots and his hands dropped away from the pack, his left bearing down on the ground, taking his weight, his right reaching for the long killing knife on his right hip.

The toes of the German's boots were pointed towards the front of the truck, so Douglas crawled silently to his right, towards the back of the vehicle, so that he would be approaching the German sentry from behind.

He crept round the rear wheels, past the tailboard, and got to his feet while still sheltered by the back of the truck. He peered round its edge and saw that the German sentry was roughly in the position he had imagined him to be, close up to the side of the vehicle, sheltered to some extent from the flying sand, his body facing the bonnet.

Douglas moved forward, his left hand thrust in front of him, his fingers hooked like talons, his right hand, clasping the knife, held back behind his right thigh and away from his body: his whole frame strung to breaking point by the conscious knowledge that he was about to kill his first man—and from behind, with deliberate intent. His left arm shot out, the forearm whipping back against the German's throat, and his right thrust forward, driving his knife into the sentry's back.

Douglas didn't know what to expect, a violent convulsion, or a sudden sagging weight—he'd never killed a man before, even from a distance. It took him long seconds of breath-held horror before he realized that what he held had no weight and little substance. His mind stumbled over the German boots—the steel helmet, its scooped up back resting against his left cheek.

He let go and stepped back, watching the straw-filled uniform sag away from him on the wires that held it up. He turned and made his way out from under the camouflaged netting, the truth still only half apparent to him. He walked towards the great petrol tank, changing the knife to his left hand and drawing his pistol, the explosives on the far side of the truck forgotten. While still yards from the side of the tank, a sudden gust of wind struck him, nearly bowling him over, and tearing away a piece of the petrol tank. With his mouth open, he watched what should have been a heavy sheet of steel glide through the air and rise suddenly as the wind caught it, swooping it away like a magic carpet. He looked back at the side of the tank, at the rectangular hole torn in its side, and at the dark void beyond.

Kostas Manou had headed for the tiered petrol drums, and before he reached them he was forced to dodge several that were blown from the top and bounded lightly past him. He dragged his sack of explosive to the foot of the pile and tapped a drum, listening to the hollow sound—it was empty. He crawled round to the back, passing the profile of stacked sand which gave to the facade of drums a substance that had deceived them from a distance. He studied what he could see of the dump's layout from where he crouched in the sand. Making up his mind, he stood up and strode past rust-encrusted vehicles till he came to a troop of anti-aircraft guns, their barrels pointing aimlessly at the sky. He jerked at the uniform of a dummy gunner and watched the figure swing back on its wires. He turned away with a shrug, grinning faintly despite his frustration. He started back to the gap in the wire but changed his mind. Instead, he headed for the wind pump, curious to discover whether or not the site had ever been a genuine petrol dump, and only used as a dummy for observation aircraft after it had been abandoned. He reached the spidery frame and crawled between its angled steel. Inside was nothing: no bore; no shaft; no pipes leading away to water-tanks. The whole complex of storage tanks, petrol drums, trucks, guns, and wind pump was as much the work of German camouflage specialists as were the dummy soldiers. He sat for a while thinking about his own position, and wondering what Douglas would consider should be the next step, and whether Leech would go along with him or make his own decision, a decision that would put Douglas in a minority of one.

He was being paid to come to this petrol dump, the one photographed by the Majabra tribesmen and marked clearly on the operational map. All right—he'd come—he'd earned his money: the fact that it was not worth blowing up was no fault of his. He sat cross-legged under the frame of the phoney wind pump. He was Greek and Douglas was English, and the English had landed their army and fought alongside the Greeks when the Nazis had thrown their weight alongside the Italians whom the Greeks were thrashing and driving back into Albania. He thought about it for a long time before shrugging and rising to his feet. Despite the emotional reaching back, there was no room for sentiment in his life, and the liking he felt for Douglas was of no consequence: if they both lived to return to safety they would probably never see each other again. He ducked under a steel girder and made his way towards the center of the raised feature. He came on the remainder of the unit standing in a bunch round Leech and Douglas, alongside one of the false storage tanks, a plywood section missing from its side and others loose and flapping in the wind. He stopped short and watched: if a decision was about to be made, he wanted to play no part in it, or be expected to support one or the other of the two men who were destined by their ethics or lack of them to be protagonists.

The wind had died down and the air was less filled with sand, visibility had increased to a considerable extent, and Kostas Manou followed Douglas' gaze as the Englishman turned and looked back to the direction from which they had all come. Through the gap in the wire, across the narrow minefield showing now a symmetrical pattern of zig-zag death, and across the half-mile of sand to the ridge from which they had started little more than an hour earlier.

He watched as Kafkarides moved away from the group, through the gap blown in the side of the dummy petrol tank and into the shelter provided by the plywood structure. Boudesh followed the Cypriot, and after a pause, Sadok and Assine. He looked to where Leech stood watching Douglas, his legs astride and his thumbs hooked in the top of his belt. He turned away and followed the others out of the wind and driving sand, conscious of disloyalty to both of the men he left outside.

Leech spoke first, his voice raised just high enough to carry to Douglas.

"We've been lucky—we shouldn't all have got back."

Douglas turned away from the desert and looked at Leech, his eyes calm and his voice level.

"I didn't come all this way to lose."

Leech's face clouded.

"Lose what? This mission's over. Masters paid me to come here. I'm here—now we go back."

Douglas tensed, his whole attitude changing.

"I give the orders, Leech. We're going to find the real dump and blow it up."

Leech grinned back at him, confident of the trump card he always carried in reserve.

"Go ahead." He nodded towards where the men sheltered in the dummy storage tank. "Give them your orders."

Douglas met the challenge of the words and Leech's cool stare by turning abruptly and striding after the men, but he was not quick enough to beat Leech through the gap in the side of the tank, and by the time he had adjusted his eyes to the gloom Leech was sitting with his back against the plywood wall alongside the others.

Douglas took a deep breath and looked at the men, ignoring Leech.

"Right. Now we're going on to find the real fuel depot. Let's go."

With the exception of Leech, all their heads turned towards him, their expressions incredulous. From Douglas, their heads swung to Leech, and despite himself Douglas followed their eyes. He saw Leech's face set in an amused smile, and watching the Dubliner's face he felt a nearly uncontrollable anger rising in his chest. Then Leech threw back his head and laughed, not a false note in the ringing gale of amusement that bounced off the plywood walls and reverberated through the empty tank, its sound exaggerated by the silence of the other occupants. Kafkarides took up the cue and his own shrill laugh drowned Leech's: Boudesh smiled, his head swinging from Leech to Kafkarides, then he started to laugh, a deep, booming note that overplayed the other two. Sadok smiled a little then joined the others, his shoulders shaking. Kostas Manou's smile was almost apologetic—Assine's uncomprehending.

Leech stopped laughing and looked round at the men.

"Let him blow up his oil depot. I'm going to find a boat. Who's with me?"

At once, the others clambered to their feet, their relief obvious to Douglas, and then they were filing past him, still laughing, shaking their heads, over-acting the part they genuinely felt. Douglas watched them go, still feeling that at some time he might have a chance of carrying them to his side—recognizing that their hammed departure carried something less than complete conviction. He swung on Leech, who had made no effort to follow the others.

"You don't care about anything—do you?"

Leech smiled gently.

"I care about you. Without me you'd have been dead a long time ago." He laughed at Douglas' surprised look. "Masters is paying me to bring you back alive."

Douglas forced the words out.

"How much?"

"Two thousand pounds."

Leech walked away, following the men, and Douglas stared after him. He watched Leech duck through the hole in the tank. He didn't doubt that what Leech had just told him was true, but the sudden revelation, coming without warning, had stunned him, slowing his thinking so that his mind groped about in an effort to come to terms with what he had learned. The idea of a British Army Lieutenant Colonel paying a criminal mercenary not to kill (or have killed) another British officer had about it an air of fantasy. He thought about Masters and wondered why he'd bothered: he was certain Masters was only interested in the success of the operation—Douglas' life meant little or nothing to the Colonel compared with an opportunity to prove his theories correct.

Douglas shook his head, looking round at the sham

interior of the false storage tank. It seemed almost poetic justice that an operation which had started out as the pipe-dream of a megalomaniac should end up at an objective that was only an empty shell.

He stepped out into the dying wind and walked down the hill to the wire. The others were already through it and making their way cautiously across the minefield. He got down and started to crawl through the wire.

When he arrived back at the camp behind the ridge, he found the vehicles loaded and ready to move. Leech was sitting in the front seat of the jeep, and as Douglas walked over to him he called out, his voice metallic with irony.

"Want a ride, captain?"

Douglas nodded silently, and Leech jerked his thumb over his shoulder towards the back of the jeep.

"Hop in."

Douglas hesitated for only a second: he had no alternative. He climbed in on top of the stores, and they moved off, Boudesh's laugh booming out above the roar of the engines.

CHAPTER 13

BRIGADIER BLORE sat behind his desk, a photograph of the petrol dump in front of him. The photograph had been taken that morning by a reconnaissance aircraft, and the blown-up version of it had been on his desk within an hour of the aircraft returning to base. Although Blore's eyes were on the photograph, he was no longer studying it. A brief glance, taken an hour earlier, had told him all he wanted to know. His present preoccupation was devoted to making the best use of the information he had gained.

There was a tap at his door and he looked up, irritably, the train of his thought broken.

"Come in!"

Colonel Masters stepped in to the room and saluted, and although the expression on Blore's face remained hard and uncompromising, his body relaxed. He hadn't expected Masters to arrive so quickly, but he was glad the Colonel had come, for without him the plan Blore had concocted couldn't be put into effect. When he spoke his voice was affable.

"Sit down."

Masters sat down, his lips pursed, his face apprehensive as he lowered himself carefully into the seat. Blore passed him the photograph without speaking, and Masters studied it.

When Blore did speak, his voice was mockingly severe.

"You seem to have failed again."

Masters looked up, his eyes meeting the brigadier's, but his expression slightly ashamed.

"I'm afraid so, sir."

Blore became suddenly almost jovial, his affability warming the room, but failing to touch Masters.

"That's all right, Masters." He paused, and his voice became brisker. "In fact, it's exactly what we want." He got to his feet and moved to a wall-map, and Masters followed him.

"Montgomery's broken through here." Blore pointed at the map, west of Alamein. "He's moving fast along the coast, here, even as far as here. By tomorrow night we'll be out of Egypt and into Libya—by the weekend —Benghazi!" He thrust his finger at the capital of Cyrenaica.

Masters' face showed amazement: the speed of the advance was something he hadn't anticipated.

"I heard it was moving, but . . ."

"Our conventional methods *do* seem to have paid off." Blore's voice was lowered till it carried a ponderous sarcasm.

The tone of Masters' reply was that of a man who knew he had lost a battle, but was not yet certain that he'd lost the war.

"Yes, quite."

Blore smiled confidently, and moved back behind his desk.

"So you'll understand that I want you to call your chaps off."

Masters' eyes swung away from his dirty fingernails and met Blore's. Real concern showing for the first time.

"I can't do that, sir. I've lost contact with them. I can receive them, but they're not getting my transmissions."

Blore's voice become suddenly aggressive.

"I've had orders to capture all fuel depots. We need them. The speed of the advance will be governed by the amount of petrol immediately available to the forward elements."

"I can understand that perfectly well, sir. But I'm powerless to do anything about it."

"Don't you have a reliable double agent?" Blore's tone became harder. "Get in touch."

Masters looked as shocked as a teacher who had just spotted a boy piddling in the classroom.

"You're asking me to inform on my own men, sir? The men I briefed and sent out there—one of them the British officer you insisted should take command?"

"Do you know any other way to stop them?"

Masters realized that Blore meant every word of what he had suggested.

"Could I have it in writing, sir?"

"No, but you'd be well advised to do it."

Masters stood up.

"I'll see what I can do, sir."

Blore looked at him once before lowering his eyes to the map on the desk in front of him.

"You do it!"

Masters walked into the shop opposite his headquarters, and spoke briefly to the barber. The Arab raised his shoulders, signifying the difficulties he would encounter in carrying out the Colonel's request. Masters spoke again, very quickly, mentioning a sum of money; at once the barber's attitude changed, and as Masters left the shop, he was already taking off his dirty apron.

Back in his office, Masters sat for a long time with his head in his hands, but at last he rose and walked over to his wall-map, his lips pursed, his face expressionless, only his eyes betraying the strain he felt.

He looked at the positions at Alamein, and then to the west at Capris Magna, but at once his eyes swung away from them to Benghazi and beyond the Cyrenian capital to the vast stretches of Tripolitania. He turned away and sat behind his desk, his decision made, the current operation no longer holding any interest for him.

He sat for two hours behind his desk, getting up only twice to examine the map on the wall for a few seconds before returning to his seat, and when the Arab was brought into him by one of his men, Masters wasted little time on the preliminaries. He didn't bargain for long about the amount of money involved, this was one item that Blore would pass without question.

He asked the Arab only if he could get through to the Germans. The method used didn't concern him, and the Arab wouldn't have told him had he asked. Satisfied that the Arab had an immediate means of communication open to him, Masters handed him a sheet of paper.

"Their wavelengths and times of transmission." He watched the Arab tuck the paper out of sight in a fold of his burnous, before continuing slowly, at dictation speed.

"They're in the vicinity of Capris Magna, heading for the fuel depot. The officer in command is 1418525 Captain R. W. Douglas, Royal Engineers. He has seven men with him." Masters paused to allow the Arab to catch up. " . . . Leech," Masters stopped again, but this time because he was thinking about Leech: he shook his head, the Irishman was the most ruthless killer and exploiter of situations he had had the good fortune to recruit; he was going to miss

Leech. "Sadok, Kostas Manou, Boudesh, Kafkarides, Hassan and Assine."

Masters watched the Arab, writing swiftly from right to left, complete the last few words and look up. Masters nodded his dismissal and the Arab slid out through the curtained door.

CHAPTER 14

THEY GOT VERY CLOSE to the small harbor town before it became necessary for them to conceal the vehicles, and when this had been done to Douglas' satisfaction, Assine led them without too much trouble through the scattered German standing-patrols. They made their way into the town on foot, relying on their Italian uniforms and the confusing movement of troops and vehicles that was going on in every one of the main streets and in any secondary road wide enough to permit the passage of a vehicle. They stopped at a small café while Assine made a further reconnaissance, and when he returned he told them of the sanctuary he had found for them.

He led them to an old ruin on top of a small hill overlooking the harbor, its remaining masonry damaged and dangerous. Looking round its interior, Douglas realized why the Germans had put it to no practical use. It was open to the sky, and every wall that still maintained a semblance of its original design was crumbling to an extent which made it so precarious that the mildest of explosions would have brought it tumbling down on the stores or men inside it.

Even from the most rewarding point of observation, they could see little in the darkness of the harbor at the foot of the hill, but they could hear uninterrupted activity and see the occasional flash of a light. They could pick out with accuracy the masked headlights of vehicles continually driving up to one particular point, and they could see by watching the dimmed lights, that the vehicles were backing and shunting, obviously loading stores of some kind before moving on to the road and heading back in the direction they had come from. Twice, the watchers in the ruin heard the clank of armor. Each time the sound lasted for upwards of half-an-hour as tanks followed the coastal road towards the east and the faint sound of cannon fire which was borne back to them from the front. Listening to the noise of the battle, Douglas tried to work out the situation from the scraps of evidence in his possession. He knew from the huge amounts of petrol he had been responsible for discharging in the weeks before he had set out on the present mission, that a big British offensive against Rommel was in the offing, but every member of the Eighth Army, through one source or another, was aware of the same thing—it was only the date and the strategy of which they were all joined in ignorance.

Sadok had been posted as a sentry; Assine was out in the town picking up what information he could; the remainder of the men were sorting out their equipment, cleaning their weapons, eating dry rations, and ever and again moving in one of the many unguarded gaps in the tottering masonry and looking out into the night.

Douglas and Leech sat together, their backs to a wall, for the most part in silence. They were waiting for the dawn and sufficient light to distinguish the lay-out of the small Arab town and the harbor facilities.

The false half-light which precedes the dawn found them both at the highest point of the ruin, waiting for the first rays of the sun to reveal to them the topography of the harbor at the foot of the hill, and when the sun rose they both studied it. They were close enough not to need field-glasses: the whole of the harbor installations lay below them as clear as a sand model used for troopless tactical exercises.

The town was very small, but the harbor installations were good, at some stage enlarged and modernized by the British when they held the town. Arab boats were plentiful in the harbor, and Leech's eyes locked on to them, weighing up the seaworthiness of each, discarding most with a small explosion of air that he forced out from between his lips.

Running right alongside the harbor was a fuel depot its size out of all proportion to what would usually be maintained by coasters plying along the German line of advance. Douglas studied the depot with a professional eye. There were no huge storage tanks which would have given the game away to the British Desert Air Force, but the cleverly camouflaged drums were stacked in tens of thousands. He watched the German trucks driving up from the east, and he appreciated the frantic haste with which they were reloaded and despatched back to the front and the roar of the guns.

Leech spoke first.

"Boats!" he said, excitement electrifying the single syllable.

And then Douglas, as if he hadn't heard the Dubliner's word.

"Petrol!"

They turned in to each other, Leech, his face set in anger as if he'd been snarled at by a toy dog.

"Forget the petrol. The minute night falls, I'm going to be on one of those boats. I feel a deal safer at sea."

Douglas nodded his head to the heavy fortifications round the harbor.

"I'm quite sure you do," he said. And Leech looked irritably back at the gun emplacements and the sentries patrolling them in force. And while he watched, his mind filling and emptying with plans to outwit the sentries and get to the sea, Assine approached them from behind, fresh back from his last scouting expedition. He addressed his report to Leech.

"Plenty boats. Too many guards. Not possible."

Deliberately, Douglas prepared the way quietly, attempting to make his suggestion sound disinterested.

"I know one way you can do it."

Leech's head swung round, his interest sharpened as nothing else Douglas could have said would have sharpened it.

"What's that?"

"You could create a diversion. Blow the fuel dump, and while they are fighting the fires you could grab a boat and get back to collect your two thousand pounds —plus."

Leech grinned.

"Are you still trying to get a medal?"

Douglas smiled back at him.

"I'll get my medal—you'll get your boat."

Leech didn't reply for two or three minutes while he studied the harbor, seeking to find another way out of the situation, but at last he agreed.

"All right," he said, "we'll give it a try."

By the time darkness fell, all their arrangements were completed, and Leech spoke briefly to Douglas.

"I'm going back to collect Sadok, and make sure the nurse is safe. I'll take Assine."

Douglas nodded. During all the time they had been in the ruined building it had been necessary that one of the unit stayed with the nurse and Hassan, now they needed every man they could muster. He watched Leech and Assine duck through a gap in the west wall, and a part of him wondered whether he would ever see either of them again. It would be easy for them to slip away, perhaps taking the ambulance with them, for Assine would never leave Hassan. He shrugged and turned back to the rest of the unit: there was nothing he could do about it.

Following Assine through the outskirts of the town and into the desert, Leech thought about the operation as Douglas had planned it, attempting to make a calculated assessment of its chance of success. He shook his head once or twice at imponderables. He had picked out the boat they were to make for if the diversion was sufficient to enable them to get to the beach undetected, but he thought that there were too many of them to get away without at least one of them being spotted. Of course, if there were casualties it would become easier. Douglas had a plan for getting back to Hassan and carrying him down to the shore, but Leech didn't give that part of the plan a thought: he had already decided to play no part in it. With Assine, he considered he might just make it out into the desert and link up with the advancing British forces. But he knew Assine would not leave Hassan, and in any case that chance was no better than Douglas' plan, for the whole area to the south would now be fluid, with units coming back from the front and regrouping before advancing again, or retiring to other prepared positions somewhere to the west. Leech laughed silently to himself; circumstances had combined so as to leave him no alternative but carrying out the major part of what Douglas had planned.

They joined Sadok at the ambulance and all climbed in the back. Leech watched while Assine bound the nurse to one of the bunks and then gagged her. He looked down at Hassan while Assine lighted a cigarette for his friend. He pointed at the nurse.

"One move out of her, and . . ." He drew his finger across his throat, and Hassan nodded up at him.

Assine kissed Hassan and put the lighted cigarette in his mouth.

They climbed out of the ambulance and started their trek back through the sand to the ruin and the rest of the unit they had left sheltering in it. Assine flitted ahead of Sadok and Leech like a wraith, every now and again melting into the desert so that the two men behind him lost sight of him for minutes at a time. Leech felt Sadok shrug as he walked alongside him, and he asked:

"Why do you jump, Sadok? What do you think about?"

The Tunisian turned his face up to Leech, the whites of his large eyes and his good teeth showing as sudden flashes in the moonlight, and he said "I was thinking, Captain, I was thinking that in the morning while it is still dark we may all of us be dead. If we live, or only some of us live—we may be dead later tomorrow. Perhaps we shall . . . all live, perhaps we shall escape. Perhaps the English will get to us before the Germans have killed us, and we'll be back again—safe in camp.

"And then I thought—what will happen to us next? Where will the Colonel send us? Where will we feel we have to go because of the money and—and something else we all know about and cannot tell to another? And I wondered, Captain, where will it all end? For you and for the English officer—for Boudesh, Kafkarides, Assine, Hassan, and—for me. I think often of these things, Captain. But tonight I think stronger."

Leech glanced quickly at Sadok, but he could see nothing of the Tunisian's face, now hidden in his burnous. With the exception of Douglas, he knew every man in the unit well, but only at a certain level. Sadok had surprised him and he was curious.

"Have you wives, Sadok?" He asked.

Sadok's face turned quickly to Leech, and then back again to the desert.

"I have one wife, Captain, one only, although the Prophet said I could have more. Other women—yes—I have other women. In Cairo, Alexandria, Qattara, and some in towns that the German general holds—but I have only one wife, and only one son. If I live I shall go back to them—to Bône." He used the French name for the Tunisian town. "I shall go back to them and we shall start a business, but of course," and he turned again and smiled up at Leech, "only if I live."

Assine came suddenly back to them, and they slid over a broken wall on the outskirts of the town, up two dark alleys less than three feet wide, across a narrow open space, and into the unit's headquarters from the south.

Douglas was adjusting the controls on the radio when Leech and the Arabs came through the wall, and he looked up with a sense of relief when he saw them. He turned back to the wireless and tapped out his message on the morse-key.

Leech went straight across to where Douglas was transmitting.

"What are you telling them now?" he asked.

"That we attack at midnight tonight."

Douglas turned back to the wireless set and continued with his message.

Five miles to the east of the harbor town, at the edge of a small olive grove south of the coastal road, a German direction-finding vehicle stood with its hood facing towards the west. The driver was in his seat, ready for a fast getaway if the British troops, fighting their way up from El Alamein, got too close. From where he sat, with the window of the vehicle down, he could hear the roar of the guns, and even the crackle of machine-gun fire.

In the back of the truck, a signals operator sat at a small table, his officer behind him holding a card in his hand with the times that Douglas was due to transmit neatly typed on it. He nodded at the operator, and the man at the table switched on the scanner fixed to the roof of the vehicle and played the knob of the receiver fractionally to the left and right of the cycle he had been given. After a minute or two of seeking, he wrote quickly on his message pad, read the finding on the scanner and added the degrees and minutes of the direction from which the message had come. He handed the pad over his shoulder to the officer behind him.

Forty miles to the west of where Douglas and his men hid in the ruined building, and twenty miles south in the desert, another German direction-finder was at work. Within minutes of his message being transmitted, both direction-finding vehicles had transmitted their readings to the German Signals Headquarters, and an officer drew two lines on the map, raising his eyebrows in surprise as he recognized the intersection where the lines crossed. It was the small Arab town in which his own headquarters were already hard at work packing equipment, loading trucks, and getting ready for an immediate evacuation which would carry them to another small town, somewhere west of Benghazi. He wrote quickly on his message pad and handed it to the operator, waiting while the message was telephoned to the German garrison commander.

With his orders issued, there was nothing further for Douglas to do but wait until midnight. He sat down with his back against the north wall and looked round at the other members of the unit, except for Kostas

Manou who was on guard, all resting in their own peculiar positions. Leech was asleep, or at least resting, stretched out on the ground with the collar of his drill jacket pulled up till it covered his ears and half his face. Douglas wondered how Leech could sleep knowing that within two hours they would all be engaged in a desperate gamble with the odds stacked heavily against them.

Boudesh lay with his shoulders and neck resting on a bulky pack of explosives; his big body was completely relaxed, only his small eyes moved, flitting from Kostas Manou looking out through the gap in the wall towards the most likely approach from the little town, to the others sitting or lying round the walls. He was wondering what the situation would offer if only two or three of them escaped—or perhaps only one, and it was himself. He wondered if he could find his way back to the ambulance and the other vehicles, although only the ambulance interested him. It would be more comfortable, and there would be plenty of room for spares in the back of it, for it held only Hassan and the nurse. He forgot about Hassan and started to think of the German nurse.

Douglas saw the smile creep over Boudesh's face, and wondered what could be amusing the Lebanese.

CHAPTER 15

THEY HAD LEFT the ruined building behind them, and now they huddled together in sparse cover only a few yards from the wire. They could see the Germans at work inside the compound, loading trucks and restacking drums under the shaded arc-lights which cast long shadows over most of the depot; whenever a work-party completed a task the light necessary for their particular work was immediately cut off. They watched the German sentries pacing their regular beats between the stacked drums, and to their left they saw the great double gates through which, every ten or fifteen minutes, the trucks came to be loaded with fuel.

Douglas tapped Kostas Manou on the shoulder and nodded towards the wire. The Greek nodded back at him and smiled, and even in the bad light Douglas recognized the sadness on the other's face. As Kostas Manou slid forward, the end of the guide-line gripped in his teeth, Douglas felt his stomach muscles tighten. Through the hours of waiting between the crumbling walls of the building they had just left, he had been strung up, feeling that any action would relax or break him. Ever present in his mind had been the possibility that Leech had prepared a palace-coup, and that at a time of their choosing they would desert him, or perhaps kill him. The only reassurance he had felt had been due to his recently acquired knowledge that alive he was worth two thousand pounds to Leech, and dead, nothing. To this knowledge had been coupled the recognition that Leech could think of no better plan to obtain his boat. The expression of sad resignation on Kostas Manou's face had brought home to him the actual physical danger of the mission, which until now had been overlayed by his apprehension of Leech and his intentions.

He watched Kostas Manou reach the wire, turn on to his back, and cut the first strand. The Greek worked quickly, but it would take him several minutes to cut a path through the wire for the others. Douglas turned his head and looked at Leech, lying alongside him, his face close to Douglas' shoulder. He turned back again and watched the Greek's progress: he had learned nothing from looking at Leech that he didn't already know. With any other man there would have been something; a meeting of eyes, a sense of shared danger; an acceptance that they were in something together, even although they might have no particular liking for each other. Leech was as near as possible to being the island complete of itself that Donne had denied could exist, and Douglas found himself following the line of thought. If the bell tolled between now and the dawn—would it be for Sadok, for himself, for Leech—or perhaps it would be for all of them?

He felt a tug on the line and passing it to Leech he eased himself forward and made for the wire. He turned on his back and humped himself through the path Kostas Manou had cut, pushing up at the lower strands to keep the barbs from catching in his clothing. Once on the other side, he jerked at the guide-line and made for the low wall lying between the wire and the stacked drums. Peering over the wall, he picked out the two German sentries closest to where he crouched, but failed to spot Kostas Manou. He waited until the two sentries met, exchanged a word or two, and turned back on their beats, walking steadily away from each other. When they were about thirty yards apart and both hidden from him by the stacked drums, he vaulted over the wall and headed in a crouching run for the cover of the nearest pile. As he reached it, he spotted Kostas Manou and felt the Greek's hand on his wrist pulling him down into the deep shadow at the base of the towering mass.

Leech felt the tug on the line and jerked his head at Sadok. He watched the Tunisian slip forward and start through the wire, and he looked at Kafkarides and Boudesh. Assine was a little apart from them, farther back, as if he were trying to maintain a link with Hassan. The Lebanese and the Cypriot would do whatever he ordered because they always saw any action he took as benefiting both him and themselves. It annoyed Leech that at that particular moment he could think of nothing better than to carry out Douglas' plan. There was another tug on the line, and Leech sent Kafkarides forward with a wave of his hand.

He despatched Boudesh and Assine at intervals, and then followed them himself. He arrived at the wall as the Senussi went over it in a gliding roll, and he waited as Assine flitted into the darkness. He watched the movement of the sentries and choosing his time he was over and into the shadow cast by the drums.

He closed up to where Douglas lay between Kostas Manou and Sadok. They conferred quickly in hoarse whispers, the imminence of the assault adding an urgent hiss to their breathed words. They made their final dispositions without argument and passed their instructions to the waiting men, and each slipped away in turn to his selected objective. Boudesh was the last to go, and as he slid away along a line of drums his foot caught a carefully laid trip-wire. The big man arrested his forward movement with the agility of a cat, throwing his weight back on to his rear leg—but he was too late.

The alarm-bells surrounding the depot clanged a strident peal, and every member of the unit froze into the shadows a split second before the arc-lights were switched on. Almost at once, two searchlights were probing the confines of the depot, and Douglas and Leech, separated only by a narrow lane between the stacked drums looked at each other, their minds racing in an effort to find a way out.

Before either had come to a decision, a voice came to them over a loud-hailer—its accent German, but the words English.

"Put down your guns and stand up please. First, come forward: 1418525 Captain R. W. Douglas, Royal Engineers."

Douglas felt his face muscles slacken and his bowels move suddenly. In the half light thrown by the arcs across the narrow gap he saw Leech frown and his eyes widen, and a sudden suspicion was allayed.

"Second: Cyril Leech."

The relief was so great that Douglas nearly laughed aloud, and he mouthed Leech's Christian name at him across the gap.

"Cyril?"

Leech grinned back to cover his embarrassment, and the voice continued through the loud-hailer.

"Now, Sadok, Kostas Manou, Boudesh, Kafkarides, Hassan, Assine. Stand up and come forward. You are surrounded. You are brave men, but there is no point that you die like heroes—for nothing!"

Douglas pointed to one of the searchlights and called softly to Leech.

"You take that light—I'll take the other." And then to Kostas Manou, the only other man he could see. "Shorten your fuses."

Leech slipped round the piled drums, and Douglas

heard his voice raised as he called to the rest of the unit.

"When we shoot the lights out, throw your charges *that* way, and we go *that* way. . . ."

And he was back in place, nodding to Douglas that he was ready.

They raised their guns and opened fire together, the bullets from their sub-machine guns smashing the roving eyes of the searchlights, and although the arcs still shone their hooded beams into the depot the sudden elimination of the stronger lights threw the area round the crouching men into a sudden darkness.

Douglas saw Kostas Manou hurl his haversack into the night, the glowing fuse inscribing a brief parabola against the sky, and then the Greek was running towards the wire, and only seconds later Douglas saw Boudesh lumber after him, his huge frame covering the ground as fast as Kostas Manou had.

The first of the charges went off, and at once a great sheet of flame climbed up into the darkness; the watchtowers stood out like stilted ants; the German gunners strained behind their sights in an attempt to separate the dancing shadows cast by the flames from the darting men; and Douglas started forward to follow Kostas Manou and Boudesh. Before he had moved a yard, he felt Leech's hand clamp like a vice on his arm and jerk him back.

"This way!"

"But . . ." Douglas started to protest, but he was jerked between a gap in the drums and pulled along in the opposite direction to the one Leech had told the remainder of the unit to take.

Sadok placed his charge and ran clear, separating himself from the explosive by as wide a margin as possible before throwing himself to the ground at the edge of the dump. He waited till his charge exploded and then stood up, calculating that even if he was spotted by the German troops they would not fire directly into the stacked petrol drums. In the light cast by the nearest arc lamp, he could see over the low wall, and he saw Boudesh drop to the ground and start to follow Kostas Manou through the wire. From the corner of his eye he glimpsed another figure dart out from the drums and head for the wall. It was Assine, and he saw the Senussi clear the wall in a smooth movement, seeming to roll over it without actually touching the brickwork. Then Assine was running for the wire. A German section came into the light cast by an arc lamp lower down the perimeter, to the left of Sadok, and he spotted them at the same moment as Assine. The guide checked his stride for a second as if to turn back; the Germans opened fire, and he continued on towards the gap cut by Kostas Manou. The first bullet hit him; he staggered to the right and then ran on, his head back, his mouth open, screaming.

"Hassan! Hassan!"

He was yards short of the wire when the hail of bullets hit him, the impact throwing him to the ground at right angles to the direction he was running in.

Sadok fired two quick bursts in the direction of the advancing Germans and melted back among the petrol drums. As he moved into the shadows cast by the burning petrol to the left and right of him, where he and Kostas Manou had thrown their charges, he saw the big gates to the dump swing open and the first of the German truck infantry drive in.

Sadok knew which boat Leech had decided would suit them best, and as he got clear of the burning petrol he changed direction, heading north to the sea through the undamaged part of the depot. At the northern limit of the dump he lay down and looked out towards the Mediterranean. He stayed quite still for two or three minutes, recovering his breath, and thinking of how the water in front of him spread without interruption for hundreds upon hundreds of miles to the west—to Bône, where his wife and son awaited his return. He took out his wirecutters and eased himself across the narrow gap to the double-apron fence. He cut his way through with quick, deft movements, shutting his mind to the possibility that the wire might be booby-trapped. Once through, he ran swiftly across the smooth sand to the sea. He had waded out till the water was washing round his knees when he heard the sound of the jackboots on the sand behind him, and he threw one quick look over his shoulder at the running Germans. He plunged on till he was thigh-deep and the first hurried shots were whistling past him. He checked and turned, knowing that his only chance was to drive the Germans to cover. He stood with his legs braced, firing back at the scattered figures on the shore, but as he emptied his magazine and started to grope for another, a burst of fire took him full in the chest and he fell forward into the sea, his burnous opening slowly and spreading across his floating body like a shroud.

Kafkarides had ignored both orders, and had neither thrown his charge nor followed the escape route indicated by Leech. His drug-warped brain had one advantage over the minds of the others: in the final analysis, when a situation was approaching the stage when it would shortly be every man for himself, he was not only capable of disregarding the safety of the others, he also recognized that Leech operated in exactly the same way. He worked his way up through the stacked drums till he was near the south-east corner, the nearest point to the wire: the charge he carried would blow him a private road to freedom.

He gauged the distance, lit his fuse, and ran out into the open to hurl the charge. As he hit the lane between the drums and the wall, a group of German infantry came round the corner and closed in on him. His hand flew up to the fuse, his intention to rip it clear of the detonator and charge, but he changed his mind, his half-closed hand concealing the glow from the Germans. Caught in Axis uniform, he was already a dead man and he knew it. His eyes staring, he grinned at the Germans as they grew closer, their weapons thrust forward. He started to laugh, the sound high-pitched and cracked, so that the Germans checked for a moment, their eyes wide. Kafkarides was still laughing when the charge exploded in his arms, blowing him and the Germans high into the air and outwards, so that pieces of them all fell in a symmetrical circle like the sparks from a roman candle.

Kostas Manou was half through the wire before Boudesh started, and his thinner body moved faster than the Lebanese could hump his bulk along. Boudesh's barrel chest caught more often on the barbs above him, and he sweated as he struggled in Kostas Manou's wake, dropping farther back with each yard he crawled.

The Greek was almost through, reaching above his head to push the last strand clear, and as he looked back over his eyebrows he saw the straddled legs of the German soldier only feet away from him. His hands stilled and he moved his head very slowly, his eyes creeping up the German's body, passing the levelled barrel of the automatic pistol, and coming to rest on the set Teutonic face and the cold eyes looking into his own. Kostas Manou smiled faintly, and his lips fluttered gently as he breathed his apology to the Orthodox Church. The German emptied half his magazine into Kostas Manou from a range of four feet, then he raised his gun, levelling it at where Boudesh had stopped coming forward and was trying desperately to hump his way back through the wire, feet foremost. His movements were too frantic and he made no progress, every angle of his body becoming entangled in the barbs. The long, sustained burst from the German's gun bounced Boudesh against the restraining strands of wire, so that his huge body heaved sluggishly under the impact like a captive balloon in a gusty wind. The last bullet hit him and he sagged in the sand, his bloodied flesh and shattered bones shrinking till he looked no larger than an average man.

In the ambulance, back in the desert behind the ruined building which had sheltered the unit in the long waiting hours before the attack, Hassan stirred on his bunk. His dull eyes lifted to where the nurse stood, her wrists strapped to the top of the bunk opposite where he lay. He looked at her face, the gag distorting her features, only her frightened eyes showing clear. He heard the sudden explosions, and he smiled. Almost at once, he heard the sustained crackle of automatic fire and he raised himself on his elbows, his eyes growing brighter with fear as he realized that the unit had been discovered and were under fire. The effort brought the blood to his mouth from his pierced lung and he sank back with it running slowly from the corner of his mouth. He looked again at the nurse, his eyes clouded and unseeing: he knew he was very near death. He listened to the continuing sound of small-arms fire, and at last groped for the gun in the blankets hugging his thigh. Twice, he tried to raise himself, each time falling back on to the bunk: the third time he remained hunched up on his left elbow. It required all the concentration of which he was capable to lift the pistol and hold it steady, aimed at the German nurse!

He looked once into her terrified eyes, and then pressed the trigger twice.

The nurse felt the thrusting thud of the bullets in her body and her breath caught in her throat as she slumped as far as the binding round her wrists would allow. Dying, she raised her eyes to Hassan and saw him start forward in the bunk, his mouth open and his eyes wide. She heard his choked cries as he called aloud.

"Assine! Assine!"

And in her final moment, before her eyes blacked out, her professionalism recognized the great gushing hemorrhage to be Hassan's last.

After they had travelled through the narrow lanes between the still intact drums to the west of the depot, Douglas and Leech crouched in the shadow of the furthest pile. Douglas was held immobile and silent by the grip on his wrist that Leech had never for a moment relaxed. They watched the last of the truck infantry come through the gate, south and only thirty yards to the right of where they lay. They listened to the automatic fire come to them in bursts, fade, restart, and then die away altogether. The gate opened again and a fire-tender came through. Leech spoke abruptly.

"Let's get out of here."

Douglas smiled in the darkness, recognizing that in a situation like the one they were in, Leech was about three jumps ahead of him.

"Aye, aye, Captain."

Leech spoke very quickly, his lips close to Douglas' ear.

"There'll be more fire-tenders. Next one in, we walk out."

Douglas found himself nodding in the darkness.

Trying to accept the advantage that the uniforms they wore gave to them.

They heard the roar of another vehicle approaching the double gates, and before it arrived Leech was pulling Douglas to his feet.

"Take it easy. Take it easy, it's our depot."

And they were walking side by side towards the opening gates. They met the fire-tender as it came through, the crew hanging on the sides, and both of them waved it past with gestures of authority. At the gate, Douglas felt his heart race and the adrenalin build up, but a wave of Leech's hand got them through, and they hugged the wall of a building on their right. Leech said, "Now," and they were through a narrow opening, making their way to the courtyard beyond it. They moved fast through the narrow lanes of the Arab town, realizing as they went that it was little more than a blown-up village. They got to an open yard with a lean-to shed, and they pushed through the goats and sat down with their backs against the mud-plastered wall. They sat for a minute or two in silence, breathing deeply. Douglas broke the silence.

"Somebody informed."

Leech didn't look at Douglas. He sat with his knees bent in front of him, staring at the opposite wall.

"Yes—Masters."

Douglas looked quickly at Leech, and his voice was surprised.

"Why should he do that?"

"To stop us blowing up the oil—they must have changed their minds."

Douglas' voice was shocked, and incredibly cold.

"If he betrayed his own men, he deserves to be shot."

Leech's reply was nearly warm with tolerance.

"You shouldn't care so much. What does it matter whether they betray you, the Germans catch you, or you trip over a mine?"

"It's a matter of principle."

"You sound like the man who gave me fifteen years!"

They both laughed together, and Douglas found himself for a moment liking Leech, and he wondered if perhaps he had learned something worthwhile from him.

The sky over their heads was suddenly alive with brilliant flashes, and to the east they heard the sound of renewed gunfire. They both turned their heads and looked up into the night.

"An air-raid?" Leech's query was uncertain.

"They're twenty-five pounders. It's the Eighth Army coming for the oil."

Leech's mouth turned down at the corners, and he grunted.

"They'll find most of it still there. We didn't do such a good job."

Douglas got to his feet and moved towards an opening in the wall, and Leech called to him softly.

"Where are you going?"

"To meet them."

"Stay here. It'll be safer in the morning."

Douglas turned back, recognizing the good sense in Leech's warning.

"It's just that I can't wait to have a word with Masters."

They laughed together for the second time in the weeks they'd known each other.

CHAPTER 16

IT WAS VERY EARLY in the morning, but Brigadier Blore was already in his office, clothed in battle-dress, ready for a move along the coast to a more advanced headquarters. He was moving the pointers on his map westwards along the North African coastal road towards Benghazi, when he heard a knock at his door, and turned towards it, his face smiling.

"Come in!"

It was Masters, still looking like a teacher on holiday in a Portuguese fishing village. He seemed uncertain as to how he would be received.

Blore advanced across the room to meet him, his hand held out. He seized Masters' and pumped it enthusiastically.

"Wonderful news, Masters."

"It is rather good, sir, isn't it?"

Blore moved away from Masters to a tray resting on a small table, his sense of well-being unconcealed, and yet at the same time strangely secretive, his lips tucking the smile in against his teeth.

"Not too early in the morning for a drink, is it?"

Masters sat down, his cheeks drawn in, his eyes on the brigadier, already pouring the drinks.

"No, sir."

"Splendid." Blore turned with Masters' drink in his hand, holding it out. "I gather your chaps got the message in time, and that the fuel-depot's in pretty good shape."

Masters accepted the whisky, a fleeting smile accompanying the look he turned up to Blore.

"Yes, it would appear so." He paused before taking advantage of the situation. What he had done went, at least to some extent, against the grain, and he wanted his reward. "By the way, sir, I did have one or two notions about stirring up a bit of trouble in Tripolitania . . ."

"You want to carry on?"

"Of course . . ."

"Good. Tell me more."

Blore picked up his own glass and stood poised with it in his hand.

"But first—here's to Monty!"

Masters stood up and raised his glass, his reservations about where the credit lay not obviously revealed.

"To victory!"

"To victory!"

They both drank to Masters' toast, and for the first time in an interview with the brigadier, Masters smiled happily. He had obtained his reprieve and was riding on the crest of a wave. The opportunity to prove his theories correct was not yet lost.

Douglas and Leech still sat with their backs against the wall of the open goat shed, listening to the constantly changing sounds carried to them from the streets of the town. They had heard for a period of several hours the constant drone of vehicle engines as the Germans pulled out. Once, the outskirts of the town had been bombed from the air. They had heard the clank of a small detachment of armor passing to the west through the desert south of where they waited. But for over half an hour they had heard nothing.

Douglas stood up, and smiled down at Leech.

"Have you got anything white?"

Leech stayed where he was and shook his head.

Douglas wandered round the open courtyard, and at last found a piece of greying fabric. He picked it up and tied it to a stick. He looked at Leech again, and taking his pistol from its holster he threw it on the ground.

"Come on."

Leech looked dubious, but he got to his feet slowly, shaking his head from side to side. He thought Douglas was being precipitate, but could find no argument strong enough to advance. Douglas spoke again, encouragingly.

"What's the matter? Anything that moves now will be British."

Leech stood looking at Douglas, his legs astride and his hands hanging slackly by his side, his face showing the wary suspicion of a wild animal.

"Just stay."

Douglas turned at the entrance to the courtyard and smiled back at the Dubliner. He laughed suddenly—liking Leech.

"Come on, Cyril, don't you want your two thousand pounds?"

Leech undid his belt reluctantly, letting it drop to the ground round his feet. He shrugged and followed Douglas through the opening.

They got to a main street, their hands and the white flag held high, just as a British tank burst through a mud wall and turned up the street away from them: another one followed it—and then nothing.

The two men lowered their hands, staring after the retreating tanks, unaware of the two scouts of the infantry patrol who cut into the street from a lane behind them.

The leading man of the patrol, a corporal, had been in the desert for a long time. He took in the two Axis officers in front of him, and the long swinging burst from his Sten gun hit them full in the back, so that they swivelled like tops before folding into the sand.

He walked to where they lay and turned them with his boot, noticing the white flag on the stick for the first time. He looked up as the young second lieutenant, fresh out from England, came up to where he stood.

"I'm sorry sir. I didn't see the white flag."

The subaltern stared at the corporal, horror at the killing fighting with the image he had of an officer's conduct in war.

"Don't let it happen again."

He turned from the scene and walked up the street in the wake of the disappearing tanks. An armored troop-carrier crushed its way up the narrow lane the infantry patrol had used, filled with laughing troops on their way to victory. In the back of the carrier a radio blasted the silence of the deserted town. The tune was "Lili Marlene," the singer, a woman, and the words, English.

How many of these Dell Bestsellers have you read?

NICHOLAS AND ALEXANDRA by Robert K. Massie   **$1.25**

THE DOCTOR'S QUICK WEIGHT-LOSS DIET
   by I. Maxwell Stillman and S. Sinclair Baker   **95c**

ROSEMARY'S BABY by Ira Levin   **95c**

THE DEAL by G. William Marshall   **95c**

SEVENTH AVENUE by Norman Bogner   **95c**

THE PRESIDENT'S PLANE IS MISSING
   by Robert J. Serling   **95c**

THE KLANSMAN by William Bradford Huie   **95c**

OUR CROWD by Stephen Birmingham   **$1.25**

THE FIXER by Bernard Malamud   **95c**

GO TO THE WIDOW-MAKER by James Jones   **$1.25**

BASHFUL BILLIONAIRE by Albert B. Gerber   **95c**

THE SHOES OF THE FISHERMAN by Morris L. West   **95c**

THE LAWYERS by Martin Mayer   **$1.25**

MY SILENT WAR by Kim Philby   **95c**

MIDNIGHT COWBOY

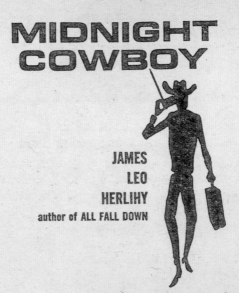

JAMES

LEO

HERLIHY

author of ALL FALL DOWN

"This is the story of Joe Buck, a loner. Joe has never known how to reach out and make contact with another human being. His only clue to communication lies in his body. Dressed up in a new cowboy outfit, he heads for New York City, where rich women will pay to possess him. MIDNIGHT COWBOY is concerned with the descent of Joe Buck into New York's nighttime dregs and of his breakthrough to feeling for someone outside of himself. . . ."
—*New York Herald Tribune*

"Brilliant . . . dazzling talent"
—*Newsweek*

Don't miss the great United Artists motion picture starring
Dustin Hoffman and Jon Voight.

DELL 75c

There will never be another spy like Philby—
There will never be another book like this one!

My
Silent
War

Kim Philby's story is that of a man who achieved the ultimate in the art of deception. He tells why he became a Soviet Agent and how he advanced to the most sensitive post in the British secret service to become the master spy of the 20th century.

"I knew him personally and was familiar with his work; and I can say with confidence that his memoirs, over that period, are factually true. . . . He is the sharpest of observers as he was the neatest of operators."

—H. R. Trever-Roper
The New York Review of Books

A DELL BOOK   95c

If you cannot obtain copies of this title at your local bookseller, just send the price (plus 10c per copy for handling and postage) to Dell Books, Box 2291, Grand Central Post Office, New York, N.Y. 10017. No postage or handling charge is required on any order of five or more books.

Here, from personal interviews
and newly declassified documents,
is the greatest, most dramatic
story of World War II . . .

The Fall
of Japan

by William Craig

The last blazing weeks of World War II
which changed the course of history.

"The most violent, shock-filled chapter
in human history. . . . *The Fall of Japan*
is virtually faultless."

—S. L. A. Marshall
The New York Times Book Review

A DELL BOOK 95¢